MW01164616

THERAPY FIX

Tina,

Thank you for your
friendship. Hope you will
enjoy the book.

Carolyn J.

THERAPY FIX

Helen Baskerville-Dukes

Edited by Anna M Costa

Cover Picture: Shutterstock Shutterstock.com

ISBN: 978-0-578-23207-2

Printed in the United States of America

Helen Baskerville-Dukes is represented by T. Fielding Lowe Company, LLC.

T. Fielding Lowe Company, LLC.

Burrillville, Rhode Island

T.Fieldinglowellc@gmail.com

ACKNOWLEDGMENTS

Heavenly Father... *You are the giver of every good and perfect gift! "I Love You"*

Husband...*Tyrone, your love and support are evident. You continue to care and push me to follow my dreams. I love you, dude!*

Mom... *You are my biggest cheerleader. You never gave up on me. Your kind words, your encouragement and support whenever needed made the greatest impact in my life.*

Sister... *Donna, thank you for keeping it real. For reading and rereading just about every single script I've written. Without a question you've read more than, 16 plays, 5 movies, 4 TV pilots and 3 books along with advice. I love and appreciate you.*

Facebook Family and Friends... *It was your likes, loves and wows that encouraged me in my daily posts, 100 posts to be exact. You all allowed me to entertain you and expressed the need for me to publish Therapy Fix. Kelly Anderson, Carol Harden Brito and you all believed in me...Thank you!*

FIVE MONTHS PRIOR

For the past few months I have only been able to sleep for maybe three or four hours each night. Nightmares of the abuse I had witnessed and sustained by my father have become almost a nightly occurrence. I would wake up choking and pulling his hands away from my neck as if it were actually happening in the here and now instead of in a dream. The abuse was serious and real... even more realistic in my dreams. There are some nights I wake up crying when my dreams play as reruns of my failed and abusive relationships, mainly with Harold. It is very difficult to talk about because it provokes immediate anxiety with constant episodes of torment that I had suffered at the hands of my father and ex-lover, Harold. Besides, I've been able to build a successful career without my past getting in the way. I don't want my past to ruin what I have built for myself; stability.

My private life is just that, private. Also, I did not want to dredge up the past with my sisters because I know there were some things that happened to them that I probably would not be able to deal with. And once I share with them what my father did to me as a child, they would feel open to sharing a stream of tightly held secrets that mirrored mine.

The day I reached out to my sister, Taylor, was different. My stomach was aching. I hoped that I hadn't developed an ulcer from the stress. There was a shadow of depression I couldn't shake. When I sat down with her, I stressed that I just wanted her to listen to me. Listen, that's it. Taylor nodded in agreement and listened intently as I spoke. The tears that formed in her eyes and dripped down her face was evidence to me that she understood me. I could see that the memories and feelings that I expressed were resonating with her. When I was finished, my breath had escaped me. I had nothing more to say. Taylor grabbed my hands.

"I would recommend you go see a therapist," she bravely suggested.

"Are you crazy?" I said abruptly. I could barely get the words out of my mouth. I didn't know what she was going to say, but I know I didn't anticipate that. "I am not crazy!" I scoffed.

Taylor said she understood how I felt and that she would be there for me. I left her feeling abandoned. I wanted to leave her with the feeling of freedom but instead I was forced to face what I had been trying to hide for years. Going to see a therapist was taboo. There had to be another way to cope.

But day after day things did not get better. I isolated myself from everyone and everything. The pain turned into anger and I felt it beginning to control me. I was barely eating. I didn't even want to bathe. After pondering the idea of seeing a therapist for months, I called Dr. Kingston Brice, who was recommended to me by a male friend. I was developing dark rings around my eyes from a lack of sleep so I thought it would be prudent to at least go and see if I could possibly be helped.

I put aside my pride and acknowledged that I needed professional help. I had decided not to take on any new clients for a while and take a leap of faith. My eyes began to moisten as I called and made the appointment. There was no turning back now.

PATIENT INFORMATION

PATIENT: Juanita Winfield

AGE: 26

OCCUPATION: Technology Specialist

COMPANY: President, Winfield Consultant Firm

DIAGNOSIS: Anxiety and Depression

INITIAL EVALUATION

1. **Trauma Sustained**
   - Childhood abuse by father
   - Abusive boyfriend relationships
2. **Mood Profile (MP)**
   - Tension Anxiety
   - Anger & Hostility
   - Sleep Deprivation
   - Decreased Appetite
   - PTSD
3. **How frequent are the symptoms?**
   - 3-5 days a week
4. **Antidepressant Medications**
   (Patient Declined)
   - Revisit in 1 month

CHAPTER 1

It's been three weeks since I have been seeing Dr. Brice. For some reason, the past few nights have been the hardest for me to get through. My next appointment is in two days and I don't want to go. All we talk about is my childhood and my bad relationship choices. I really want to have a normal conversation with Dr. Brice. But he always manages to keep the focus on my medical and mental condition. I know it is his job, but still.

As I sit in my kitchen, tapping my fingers on the counter and picking through my salad, I realize I do not feel as though therapy is really helping me out. "Why do we have to meet so many times? And why do I not feel like I am getting better?" I thought to myself.

There was nothing else going on in my life, except for... well, nothing. I had nothing to distract me from this. I took a deep breath. I cannot even convince myself not to go to therapy. Well, I guess I will continue to see Dr. Brice and appease him every now and then to make him feel as though I am making real progress. However, I am not ready to tell someone that I do not know every single detail of what has happened to me throughout my life. Maybe that is why I don't feel as though I'm getting better. Sigh... I am not ready.

SEVENTH APPOINTMENT

As I walked through the doors, Diane, the building's receptionist yelled excitedly, "Hello Juanita!" Diane was chewing and smacking her gum like a horse eating hay. Chomp… chomp… chomp. She was grinning from ear to ear with red gum clamped between her pearly white teeth.

As I focused on the gum, I immediately thought of my grandmother Mae. What would she say every time I would chew gum in her presence?

"A lady doesn't chew gum" were her exact words. Meanwhile, she would sit with her legs cocked wide open smoking a cigarette. What irony! She always kept Grandpa Teddy's hunting knife on the table right next to the beautifully engraved crystal ashtray he had given her for their first anniversary. I dare not mention Grandpa's knife to Grandma Mae again.

The first and last time I ever questioned the purpose of her leaving the hunting knife on the table, she peered into my eyes and slowly put her hands on it. I waited for an answer. We played the staring game for about 30 seconds before I realized something was really wrong. At that moment, I no longer wanted to know why she kept the hunting knife there; I just wished that I had never asked that question. I was truly frightened for the first time in my life around her, so I ended the staring contest with a softly spoken, "Goodnight" and "I love you!" As I started to walk away, I saw her hand ease away from the hunting knife.

I could hear Diane still talking in the background. I was trying to focus on what she was saying, but I could not stop thinking about Grandma Mae and that hunting knife.

The sound of Grandma Mae's turquoise slippers shuffling on the hardwood floors became extremely loud. She would be up all night and into the early morning pacing the floors and talking to herself. I wanted to throw out those dingy, old slippers. Those dirty old slippers had the cushions hanging out where the towel-like material had worn down and ripped at the bottoms. However, throwing those slippers in the trash would have been impossible because she was always wearing them.

By day, Grandma Mae was very loving with an uncontrollable smile telling me how grateful she was that I had come to stay with her. By night, once dinner was over, she would barely hold a conversation with me. Besides the floor pacing and talking to herself: she would sit at the table filling the house with cigarette smoke and watching reruns like some type of ritual. Come to think of it, I don't think she even really slept. I would wake up early the next morning and she would be awake, bright-eyed and bushy tailed like she slept on a Posturepedic mattress for ten hours.

I wanted so desperately to dismiss these thoughts because the memories were painful and complicated. As the tears began to fall from my eyes, I felt someone touch my shoulder. The touch startled me.

"Juanita, Juanita," Diane said with a bit of hesitation in her voice.

I could see the concern in her face but I couldn't say anything except for, "Get your hands off of me!"

Diane leaped back and softly muttered, "Juanita, it's me Diane. Juanita, are you okay?"

I responded in a calming tone, "Yes. I just have a lot on my mind."

"Have a seat. Dr. Brice will see you shortly," Diane responded with a smile.

I smiled back and apologized for shouting at her. She didn't seem phased at all by my sudden outburst. They probably get a lot of sudden outbursts from patients waiting to go up to Dr. Brice's office. Diane is always bubbly and she reminds me so much of my sister, Taylor, who is tall, thin and very outgoing. However, under all that bubbliness, Taylor has a lot of secrets.

I found Taylor's diary in a stack of books she was donating to Camp Street Ministries. She had asked me to drop off some of her old books with the things I was going to give away. I went through the books first, just in case there was something I wanted to read. There it was, amongst the other books, a thick black covered book. The black book did not have a book title or even an author's name printed on the outside that I could see or feel. I curiously opened it. I don't think she knew her diary was on the same shelf as the books she wanted to donate. I opened it to a random page. I began to read. August 15th, he came into my room and stood over my bed. I opened one eye and watched him unbuckle his belt.

I gasped and put my hand over my mouth as I shut the diary quickly. I didn't want to read anymore. MONSTER!!!!!

"Juanita, Dr. Brice can see you now!" Diane exclaimed.

I thanked her, walked to the elevator and headed up to the 14th floor. I've been going to therapy for two months now and I truly find it amusing and liberating because I'm able to talk to someone about my past... at least some of it.

I couldn't wait to see Dr. Brice again. He is the only reason I've come back. At our first meeting, I wasn't expecting to see this very attractive man that stood about 6'1". Not too short and not too tall. "Just Right". His skin tone was like Middle Eastern dark, smooth and just sexy. His skin looked so soft, too. He has black, curly, silky hair and an amazing smile with an unforgettable dimple on his left cheek. I could tell he worked out too. Whenever he lifted his arm to run his fingers through his hair, his muscles strained the seams of his fitted button up shirt. He was positively dreamy! As I thought about him, I could smell the bold and enticing cologne he wore. It just did something to the hairs on the back of my neck. I thought doctors weren't supposed to wear cologne so that it would not trigger any type of hurtful memories or behaviors from their patients? I'm glad he does because it makes my appointments that much more enjoyable. The first time I met him there was this "vibe". I can't explain it but it was the way he looked at me. Okay, maybe it was my hormones acting whacky. However, when I first walked in, Dr. Brice tilted his head to the side and smiled. I returned the smile and extended my hand to shake his. His hand was soft and his handshake firm. It took everything I had to stay focused. I wanted him to take me seriously and not think of me as some sex object like other men do. He told me to take a seat so we could get started. As I turned to sit, out of the corner of my eye, I could see him looking me up and down. That is just what I wanted him to do. The mauve blouse I was wearing slightly showed my cleavage and the black pencil skirt fit me like a glove. My flower printed 3" heels showed off my toned legs and defined ankles. At 5'8" and weighing exactly 132 pounds, that day I felt like a model and I knew I would turn a head or two... including Dr. Brice's.

The elevator stopped on the third floor. The door opened and this older woman, who looked as if she was in her fifties, got on the elevator. She reached in front of me and pushed the button for the fourth floor. She could've climbed up the stairs in the time it took for her to wait for the elevator to come to her stop and take her up just one floor. I looked down at her feet to avoid eye contact. I chuckled inside. Now I see why she took the elevator. Her bunions were protruding out of her opened toe shoes. We stood side-by-side as I watched her watch me through the reflection on the stainless-steel doors. My ex-boyfriend Harold would do crazy stuff like that. When he wasn't looking directly at me, Harold would always look for something that could act as a mirror so he could watch my every move through the reflection.

One time we were at the ATM. He was withdrawing money. I was standing behind him when some random guy walked by me and said, "You're beautiful." Harold pushed me to the side and chased the guy down the street yelling out all types of obscenities at him. When Harold made it back to me, he insisted that I was flirting with the guy and he should leave me at the ATM to walk home.

"I wasn't flirting with him," I said. Harold slapped me down to the pavement. I couldn't believe he hit me. I kept stumbling as I was trying to get up, but I couldn't catch my bearings. He reached his hand out to help me up. As soon as I slightly gripped his hand, he let go of mine and I fell to the ground in complete embarrassment.

"I saw you looking at him through the silver plate on the ATM machine!" Harold angrily yelled.

The elevator stopped on the fourth floor and the lady quickly slipped off her shoes. My feet were hurting just looking at hers. She exited the elevator. Just as the door was about to close, a hand stopped it. I gasped and jumped when the sudden jolt of the elevator startled me. The door opened and this man looked directly into my face with an angry expression. He walked into the elevator and there was a woman following him crying. He barely waited for her to get in the elevator before pressing the eighth floor button. He cleared his throat before yelling at her.

"Gina, stop crying stupid and hurry up and get on the elevator," he said it in a demeaning tone.

His behavior was disgusting and unnecessary. "What a dirtbag!" I thought to myself.

"I'm sorry Gilbert!" Gina said as she continued to quietly sob.

I made eye contact with Gilbert again. He gazed deep into my eyes. That is when I remembered who he reminded me of. He was Harold and I was Gina, the victim. I suffered through years of abuse. All in the name of love. What did I do wrong to deserve the treatment I got at the hands of men? I don't know. I would probably never know. It haunts me still to this day, hence my therapy appointment. I'm not attracted to it, but I do believe I attract it. Some people say, "Well, just leave!" Well if it was that easy I would, but what about when I was a child? I felt my eyes filling up immediately with tears. My heart started racing.

I was under Harold's control at one point in our relationship so I know how hard it is to let go. I refused to show Gilbert fear on the elevator so I waited for him to turn his eyes from mine before I looked away. Then I looked at Gina and I prayed she read my stare. "You can walk away. You can do it," I said silently to her through my eyes. The elevator finally made it to the eighth floor. Gilbert grabbed Gina by the arm and forced her off the elevator. She gave him a dirty look and he smacked her in the face. This was the first time in my life seeing a man casually abuse a woman in public. BULLY!!!

I don't ever recall this many elevator encounters on my way up to Dr. Brice's office. My phone rang. I fumbled through my purse looking for it. Finally, I found it. As I was pulling it out, the phone clip got caught on the purse strap, causing a few items to fall out onto the floor. I lost the call. I bent down to pick up my things when the elevator door opened to the twelfth floor. No one was there waiting to get on. They must have caught another elevator.

As I quickly put my things back into my purse, the elevator door closed and my phone rang again. I looked to see who was calling. Harold! Love is certainly a feeling that isn't that easy to overcome. I know I shouldn't answer the phone and I will not.

Harold and I are not "an item" as the old folks would say, but I do desire to see him sometimes. It's been over a year since we have broken up; however, we do see each other every now and then.

Harold called me about three weeks ago out of the blue, which led to him coming over again. I didn't ask who was at the door that day when the doorbell rang, I just opened the door and there he was standing there with a faint smile. Using his deep and mesmerizing voice Harold said with slight desperation in his voice, "Juanita, I really need to talk to you." I asked him what he was doing here. He said he had to see me. I looked into his eyes and I could tell that there was something wrong. I was hesitant about letting him in, but I was anxious to know what he wanted. Plus, he just looked so doggone yummy.

I fixed him a cup of coffee just the way he liked it and sat across from him. We stared at each other for a few seconds, and then he put his head down and began to cry.

The elevator jolted to a stop as it reached the fourteenth floor, which brought me back to reality. The door slowly opened and Maureen, Dr. Brice's personal secretary, greeted me and said, "Dr. Brice is running late so please take a seat."

While waiting for my appointment, I had this uncontrollable need to go to the restroom due to the new waterfall hanging on the wall in the waiting room. Someone wasn't thinking when they bought it. I couldn't take it any longer. I had to go. Maureen smiled at me as I passed her and headed straight to the restroom.

The restroom fragrance was new and inviting. It's so funny how scents trigger memories. However, this memory I didn't want to visit. I try not to think of my mother, but that smell was all too familiar.

> One Christmas season, my mother brought home a jar candle from Waxed Candle Shop that smelled like Christmas cookies. She put it on the stovetop to burn.

"Nope, nope, I'm not going there," I said to myself in an angry tone. I have some great memories of her. I try my hardest to bottle up every good moment with my mother. I'm afraid those memories may not bring me as much joy as they once had.

I flushed the toilet and washed my hands. I tried not to look in the mirror but I couldn't avoid it this time. I could see the hurt in my eyes even when I smiled. I saw my mother in my face. My father was to blame. The late-night torturing, the ice baths, random back slaps and threatening to shave her head bald if she folded his clothes the wrong way. It all had stripped her of her beauty. I've learned to do my hair and get dressed without really looking in the mirror for eight years so how did I let it happen today?

As all these thoughts and memories swirled in my mind, I could literally hear voices. I'm not going crazy. Am I?

I didn't realize I could hear Dr. Brice through the restroom wall. I pressed my ear close to the wall so I could hear clearer. I heard the tension in his voice. "What did he do to you?" Dr. Brice asked firmly. Who could he be talking to? There was a brief pause. "You can't continue to allow him to treat you like this!" Dr. Brice takes a few steps. I can hear the thumbing of his shoes as he walks. Then he plops down on his sofa. It was a familiar sound that I have made quite a few times when I have my weekly meetings. I don't want to hear anymore, but the juiciness of this conversation has my ear glued to the wall. What has gotten him all riled up? Dr. Brice sighed and said, "I'm trying to help you, but you won't let me! I have a client," exclaimed Dr. Brice. "I'll stop by after work." Dr. Brice said in frustration and then hung up the phone.

I left the restroom holding the phone to my ear as if I was having a conversation with someone. I did not want anyone to think I was eavesdropping. As soon as Maureen saw me, she signaled that I could go into Dr. Brice's office.

I walked in and saw that Dr. Brice was still troubled by his conversation. I smiled and greeted him as if I was the therapist and he was the patient. I wasn't ready to tell him anything new. I wanted to keep up this game of charades as long as I could. Mainly, I just like seeing him. He is so charismatic. And now I am very intrigued by his phone conversation so I needed to do some investigating.

Dr. Brice began with his normal question, "Did you get any sleep last night?"

"A little," I responded as I walked around the sofa. I glanced over at him. I could see he was doodling on his pad. He wasn't really listening to me. I wanted to question him about the conversation I overheard. As I was pondering how I was going to frame my question, I started to ask him who got him so upset, but I could not get the question out in time before he asked me to sit down.

"You're making a little progress, Juanita," he said passively.

I closed my eyes tightly so that he couldn't tell I was totally annoyed by his textbook approach. I opened my eyes and saw that he was looking back at me. I could see he was looking right through me as he asked his next question. If I questioned him about his lack of engagement today I might never get close enough to find out what's going on with him. I continued to answer his questions. Basically, I gave him the answers he would like to hear until my time was up. I wanted his complete attention but the "person" he was on the phone with still had his total attention. I didn't like that.

After I left my therapy session, I stopped to get a coffee at the café across the street from Dr. Brice's office. The line was incredibly long and of course I waited impatiently. I don't know why I was in such a hurry because I had nowhere to go. About eighteen minutes later and one person away from being able to read the pastry labels in the glass case and place my order, I heard my name called. I immediately recognized my brother's voice. I quickly turned around anticipating seeing his crooked smile and thick, curly black hair.

"Juanita," Aaron repeated when our eyes connected.

I haven't seen my brother in almost three years. Sometimes, I would run into people we know and they would tell me that they have seen him around. It was very comforting knowing that he was still alive. But to witness him today is beyond a blessing. Aaron's clothes were tattered and his fingernails were disgusting. His hair was very matted. He was almost unrecognizable. There was this sadness that I have never seen in his eyes. His once glossy, vibrant green eyes are now dull holding pain and a cry for help. He looks so frail and he smells like garbage... that doesn't matter because I was glad to see him.

He began to cry like a five-year-old. After Grandma Mae died, he started popping pills. I'm witnessing all of the ill effects from the years of his apparent drug abuse. I could see the streets had won.

"Aaron, please let me buy you something to eat or get you a cup of coffee," I offered.

He put his head down and whispered, "Thank you, Sis."

I could barely hear him because his voice was distorted from his crying. I wrapped my arms around him and hugged him fiercely. I felt his tears soak through my blouse onto my shoulder. I began to cry inside because I missed him so much. He was just a baby when... it's so complicated and I am not going to let those thoughts take up any space in my mind right now.

I heard a moan in my ear. I felt Aaron become heavy and then collapse in my arms. My heart began to beat quickly.

"Aaron!" I shouted. "Call 911! Someone, please, call 911!" I cried out. "Aaron, can you hear me? Answer me Aaron." I frantically screamed while shaking him. "I don't think he is breathing. Does anyone know CPR?" I asked desperately. No one responded. I know he looks like a bum but he's my brother. I glanced to my right and I could see a woman on her phone with a look of desperation on her face. "Would anyone speak up if he had on an Armani suit?" I cried out. Over to my left there were three people watching me hold my brother.

Someone yelled out, "The ambulance is coming! They've dispatched the ambulance!"

I was very relieved as I continued to cradle Aaron. It took the ambulance forever to come. After a few minutes that felt like hours, I could finally hear the sirens getting louder and louder as the ambulance got closer.

An older man squatted down next to me and said, "I don't know what to do, but I'm here with you."

His words comforted me. I sat on the floor holding and rocking Aaron in my arms. That is how my mother would hold him after my father had kicked or punched him for not taking the trash out before he had gotten home. Aaron went through a lot. He's been punched in the face, kicked in the back, pushed to the floor, choked and smacked around since he was eight years old. Well, at least that is the age I remember the start of his abuse. I don't know... maybe I blocked out anything before then.

All orders were stopped as everyone waited around to see what would happen next. I began to sing, "He's got the whole world in his hands. He's got you and me brother in His hands. He's got the whole world in His hands". That was the first thing that came to mind. It was one of Aaron's favorites songs.

> *There were nights Aaron couldn't sleep. He would just lie in the bed for hours tossing and turning. My mother would go into his room. I could hear her singing to him. When she finally stopped singing, I knew he was asleep.*

Oh, how I wished she were here to cradle him that way right now.

"Ma," Aaron moaned.

I heard a gasp in unison by some of the customers standing around waiting to see if Aaron was alive. A sigh of relief came over me just knowing he wasn't dead. I was overwhelmed by emotions that instantly overcame me. I closed my eyes and exhaled loudly. Then I slowly opened them. Just to fix my gaze on Dr. Brice's building. And there he was standing in the front of his building quarrelling with an older woman, who was sitting in a car. She was crying as he was pointing his finger in her face. "What is going on?" I thought to myself. I put two and two together. That was the same woman he was yelling at on the phone that I had overheard while I was in the bathroom just before my appointment.

The ambulance arrived and the EMTs quickly began administering help to my brother. Aaron was dehydrated and extremely malnourished. They put him in the ambulance and transported him to Rhody Hospital.

CHAPTER 2

Aaron looked worn and tired as I stared at his skeletal face. At least he will get the proper nourishment he needs being that they were going to keep him in the hospital for a little bit. His assigned doctor and current nurse were very sympathetic and accommodating to his needs.

As I stood by Aaron's bedside and watched him. I could only imagine the pain he's been carrying around for such a long time. Everyone handles situations differently. I patted my eyes dry again from the tears that kept coming. I breathed a deep sigh.

As he slept, he talked and moved around a lot. I just could not stop crying. My eyes were hurting from wiping them so much. I braced myself against the wall and just stared back at him. I looked over my brother's frail body and the keloid scar on his leg caught my attention. Here I go again with a faucet of tears streaming down my now raw cheeks.

That day the dog had used the bathroom in the house. My father was so angry that he went in his toolbox and pulled out a pair of pliers. I watched him turn the stove on and put the pliers on the pilot until they were red-hot. My father walked over to Aaron and then clamped the hot pliers on Aaron's leg.

Branding him for life. Aaron closed his eyes and groaned through his teeth.

My father was a sick man. Aaron hadn't let the dog out because my mother told him that she would take the dog for a walk when she got home so that Aaron could get his homework done.

Who does this? That was the last straw! I questioned why my mother stayed with my father so long so many times? It's easy to say what you'll do in a particular situation until you're in it.

It was time for me to go home. I had been at the hospital all day. My youngest sister, Shanice, was on her way to the hospital to sit with our brother so I could go home. I wanted to shower and escape this familiar nightmare. I picked up Aaron's bag of dirty clothes and wondered why he had chosen this path. Why had he alienated himself from his siblings? I kissed him on his forehead like my mother used to do every night. I wanted Aaron to feel safe. We needed to feel safe!

As I was leaving his room, I was startled as Aaron yelled out, "No Daddy, you're burning me!" Then he whimpered and continued to sleep. I felt the anger flaring up inside of me. I clenched my hands into tight fists so tightly that I knew I would have fingernail impressions in my palms. I could feel the heat rise up the back of my neck. I was beyond tears at this point, remembering what happened next.

I remembered clearly when my mother came home that day and said to my father that Aaron probably deserved to get whipped. Aaron was a wild child, but there is no way of heating up a pair of pliers on the stove and then clamping them on human skin as justifiable punishment. I couldn't believe what I was hearing! How could the woman who was supposed to be protecting us side with this monster? I saw my father smirk. That made me even more furious. If that was the last time I saw him I wouldn't lose any sleep. Hearing my mother take sides with our father was devastating. How could she betray Aaron like that? "Would I be next?" I thought to myself. Later that night I started packing all of our bags. This was it! We were out of this crazy, dysfunctional house. I woke up Shanice, Taylor and Aaron and told them to be as quiet as possible. Shanice had developed this cough a couple of days before and once she started getting dressed it surfaced. I was so nervous because I did not want her to wake up our father. I told her to cough into her favorite teddy bear, Oscar, so our father wouldn't hear her. I had neatly packed bags for everyone including toothbrushes and toothpaste. I made sure to have all of this together before I even woke them up. I had a plan. We were ready to leave when Taylor decided she wanted to give Mom a kiss goodbye. I couldn't tell her no. To appease her, I told her she could kiss Mom later. Shanice, Taylor, Aaron and I were ready and headed to the door. I was last to leave to make sure no one was left behind. Aaron opened the door quietly and before we could get out without waking anyone up, my father...

"Juanita, why don't you go home for the night?" Shanice said. I relaxed my hands. I looked down and noticed that there was blood on my left hand from clenching my fist so tightly. I thought I had everything under control but apparently not. Shanice looked at my hand, but she didn't say a word. Why didn't she? Instead she just hugged me tightly and said, "Everything will be alright." I exhaled and squeezed her back trying not to get any blood on her.

Shanice was very strong. Sometimes that scared me. There were plenty of nights Shanice, Taylor and I would stay at each other's houses because we didn't want to be alone. Struggle can either bring you together or tear you apart. We would sit up and talk about a lot of things except for what we experienced as kids. As soon as one of us brought up a horrific event, one of us would gracefully change the subject.

That's probably why I'm in the predicament I am in now. However, we had each other but my brother Aaron didn't have anyone that could identify with the emotional trauma he was exposed to as a male child.

I left Aaron's room and went straight to the restroom. I turned on the faucet and started washing my hands. I looked at myself in the dirty bathroom mirror and cried some more. I remember how my mother used to cry all the time. These thoughts are very painful.

> I would listen to my mother and wonder what she was crying about until I asked her one day. She was sitting outside in the backyard one evening crying in the cold. I walked up to her and hugged her. "Ma" I said.
>
> "What is it Nita?" she softly replied.
>
> "Ma, why are you always crying?" I asked in a concerned manner. She avoided the question by telling me I wouldn't understand.
>
> Months later I woke up in the middle of the night with an upset stomach. I lay in the bed tossing and turning for about twenty minutes before I decided to get up. I went downstairs to ask my mother for something to ease my upset stomach but I couldn't find her anywhere around the house. I heard the front door

open so I hid because I didn't know if someone was trying to break into the house. I was surprised to see that it was my father coming in. Right before I was getting ready to come out from where I was hiding, I became curious as to why he was out so late, so I stayed in my hiding spot. He walked right past me and he didn't even notice me. He smelled weird. "I'm sick of this," he grumbled to himself. He went right to their bedroom and closed the door behind him, but it didn't close all the way.

I tiptoed to their room and I noticed that my parent's bedroom door was cracked open. Their bedroom door is never opened or unlocked at night. If we needed my mother or father we had to knock because we were forbidden to just walk into their room. If we did, there was a heavy price to pay. I peeked through their bedroom door but my mother was still nowhere to be found. He walked over to the closet and opened the door. There was my mother sitting in the closet on the floor in the dark. She looked terrified. "What is going on here?" I seriously thought to myself.

"Let's go now!" my father exclaimed in a harsh whisper. The look of terror was on my mother's face as she slowly got up from the closet floor. I could see *that she was crying and afraid. All of a sudden, my father grabbed her by the arm and yanked her out of the closet and onto the bedroom floor.*

"Why do you keep doing this to me? Ever since we've been married you've locked me up in this closet when you get drunk," she asked in a meek tone. I could hear the fear in her voice.

What kind of sinister act was this? How come I didn't or couldn't see that this was happening to my very own mother? WHY????... I just wanted to scream at the top of my lungs.

A pale, short and stocky woman entered the restroom. She smiled at me so I smiled back. There was pain in her face as she mustered up the strength to be cordial. It was clear that she had been crying because her nose was red and her eyes were bloodshot. She slowly walked past me and went into the bathroom stall. I turned and continued cleaning up my bleeding hand. I wrapped it with paper towels and walked out of the restroom. I grabbed some gauze bandages and tape as I left the hospital and headed to my car.

I plopped in the driver's seat and sighed deeply. "My life is falling apart. I need to go to church," I mumbled to myself. My therapist only listens to me because he's getting paid to do it. I turned the music up and laid my head back and closed my eyes. I felt like my life was closing in on me and I was falling into a black hole. I gripped the steering wheel as tight as I could with the hand that wasn't bleeding. I was holding on but I kept falling into this mentally depressed state. I shook my head in hopelessness. While I'm being strong for everyone who is being strong for me?

I was startled by a knock on the passenger window. I almost had a heart attack. It was Dr. Brice. "What is he doing at the hospital?" I thought to myself. What does he do with his free time? I was about to roll down the window when he motioned for me to unlock the door so he could get in. "Is he crazy?" I said under my breath. I turned my head away from him and wiped my eyes. He knocked on the window again and I rolled down the window.

"Juanita, can I get in?" Dr. Brice asked.

"Of course," I unlocked the door and let him in. Who wouldn't?

"What are you doing here?" Dr. Brice questioned.

I smiled and said jokingly, "I'm not paying you for this session." I am very reluctant to tell him why I'm sitting in the hospital's parking lot crying.

He chuckled and asked, "Seriously, Juanita, are you okay?"

"I'm trying to get myself together, Kingston!" I exclaimed. He had a surprised look on his face when he heard me call him by his first name.

Oh, his name is almost as sexy as he is. Just saying Kingston's name made me think about him being more than my psychologist. Dr. Brice is a few years older than I am, which is great because I don't like younger men. I found out how old he was at my first session. A week before his birthday I overheard Maureen, his personal assistant, on the phone ordering a cake. Insisting that the bakery put thirty-two candles on it. The following week, at my third appointment, there was this beautiful cake sitting on his desk in a box. It hadn't been touched. He offered me a piece but I declined. Why no candles? Why hasn't it been eaten? Not even one piece. Why was he acting as if it all didn't matter? Very bizarre...

I was startled when Dr. Brice reached over and touched my shoulder. It was rather awkward but I just played it off like I was cool with it.

"I apologize. I didn't mean anything by it," he said as he quickly snatched his hand back.

I chuckled and told him not to worry about it when in all actuality I wasn't cool. Dr. Brice slowly moved his face closer to mine. I was about to smack him when he suddenly began sniffing close to my lips like a hungry dog looking for a bone.

"What are you doing?" I asked disapprovingly while pushing him away.

He laughed and said, "I just wanted to make sure you weren't drinking."

"Really Kingston?" I replied as I sucked my teeth. "What are you laughing for?"

"I'm laughing because you called me Kingston twice," he said amusingly.

Oh, that laugh sounded all too familiar.

> I stayed home from school one day because I was sick. I heard my father come in. He didn't know I was home and nor did I want him to know. I don't know why he was home early from work this day, but he was acting very strange. My sister, Taylor, had just walked in from school like she normally did. She usually arrived from school forty-five minutes before the rest of us. My father shouted from the back, "Who is that?"
>
> "It's Taylor," she replied.

"Come here!" my father yelled out to her. I heard Taylor pause and exhale. Then she walked toward my mother's room.

After about a minute I heard Taylor scream, "What are you doing?"

My father responded with that same laugh Dr. Brice had. I didn't know what was going on but I wasn't about to wait and hear so I coughed really loud. I think they heard me but I wasn't sure. I coughed again to make sure my father and Taylor heard me. My father came out of the bedroom and as he got closer to my room every step he made became louder and louder. I was so nervous I couldn't stop shaking. My father paused outside my door for a moment. Why did he wait? Then he slowly opened my door. I know he looked in to see what bed was occupied. "Juanita," he called out. I didn't answer because I didn't want him to know I heard him. I tried my best to stop shaking. He walked over to my bed and placed his hand on my forehead. "Juanita, are you okay?" he whispered. I still pretended I was sleeping. Thank God I was a hard sleeper anyway so I don't think he worried too much about whether I heard him. He turned to leave so I coughed, moaned *and then turned over. He waited there for a few seconds and then left my room.*

"Well, are you going to tell me why you are here?" Dr. Brice asked. Dr. Brice looked at me as if he was waiting for something. He really wanted to know why I was at the hospital. I decided to tell him because I did not think he would stop asking.

"My brother was rushed to the hospital today," I replied as I looked down at his hand, which appeared to be moving closer to my leg. When I'm around him I feel this rush of attraction. I've never felt like this around anyone. Since the first day I met him, it was like a game of cat and mouse rather than trying to get myself through this depression. I wanted to tell him everything from the start, but once we began meeting, I wanted to be there and if I told him everything then that would end our session... end us.

"Do you need me to do anything for you or do you need to talk? " Dr. Brice said. "I'm here for you," he finished.

"I can handle this," I said confidently. Why did I not say yes? I do need him. I do want to talk. Now that he knows that Aaron is in the hospital, he is going to want to talk about him at our next session. Wait a minute. Why is Dr. Brice here at the hospital? Dr. Brice opened his mouth to say something but I needed to control this conversation.

"Juanita," Dr. Brice said before I interrupted him.

"What are you doing at the hospital?" I asked him. But instead of answering my question he just keeps looking at me as though he is waiting for me to say more about me being at the hospital.

"I'm waiting on a patient here," he finally answered, adjusting his body in the passenger seat. I don't believe him. For some very strange reason, I think he is following me. I feel more like a detective than his patient. I was out of words. I really wanted him to say how he felt about me because I know there's something there. It's the way he looks at me and the way he interacts with me.

We sat in the car for an entire minute saying nothing before Dr. Brice broke the silence by telling me if I needed to see him sooner to make an appointment. While he was talking I heard a car pull up beside mine. I watched Dr. Brice glance over my shoulder but I refused to look so I kept eye contact with him. An annoyed look appeared on his face as he looked back at me. Dr. Brice cracked a smile and touched my hand. In a soft, friendly voice he said, "I'll see you next week." Then he winked at me and melted my heart.

"You can see me tonight!" I wanted to scream out. When he touched me, I felt like pulling my panties off. Of course, I could not share that with him. I wanted him to touch me, kiss me or give me that look that guys give the woman when they know that they are with the right one. Why was he holding back?

I watched him get out of the car, then I turned to see who had pulled up next to me. It was the same woman he had been arguing with earlier that day across from the coffee shop.

Dr. Brice got in the car with her and I saw him look at me as if to say, "Help!" As I watched them drive off, he wouldn't even look at her.

"How do I find out who she is? Is he into older women?" I wondered. As they drove away, I wanted to know what his agenda was? Why does he need to touch me? Why is he so nice to me? You see this is the reason why I'm alone. People come across as innocent and loving; then, once you are hooked they turn into demons. I still have reservations about being in a relationship because I worry about someone treating me the way my father treated my mother or the way Harold treated me.

I started the car and drove off. I had all these depressing thoughts meeting in my head that I forgot all about Aaron. "I am an emotional train wreck," I mumbled to myself as I began to cry again. "Where is Aaron going to stay when he gets out of the hospital? Where was he staying before? Will he need to see a therapist too? Will he go look for a job? One thing at a time," I whispered to myself. I have a tendency to overthink things. Aaron's situation was very complex and I just want to make sure Aaron was going to be okay when he left the hospital.

On my way home I stopped at a traffic light and saw some young boys playing basketball. They were wearing Project Night Vision t-shirts. "Hey Mr. Dennis. What's up Mr. Dennis?" I heard a few kids yell out as a dark skinned, well-dressed man walked up to them. The man greeted the boys with handshakes and a great big smile. While he was conversing with the boys, a car pulled up beside mine.

The driver rolled down the window and yelled out, "Kobi, we need to talk!"

"Ok, you know where my office is," Kobi yelled back as they both waved bye to each other.

Aaron was very good at basketball. People would always make it a point to come out, watch him play, or even challenge him. He was even being scouted by Providence College. Basketball was Aaron's way of escaping the beatings from my father. When my father heard that Aaron was being scouted, he was so proud. The last game my father was ever permitted to attend was the one where he brought in a bat.

I closed my eyes tightly to avoid the anger that was rising up inside of me that had been trying to hold my happiness hostage for most of the day. Why is everything triggering these painful memories all of sudden? I began to bang on the steering wheel with all my might. "Beep...beep", a car horn tore me out of my musings. The driver behind me impatiently blew the horn again encouraging me to go. I hadn't noticed that the light had turned green. I wanted to give the driver behind me the finger but that wouldn't be lady-like. I was about to take off when one of the kids from the basketball court ran across the street.

My mother, father and I were at Aaron's championship game. You could clearly see that one of the referees and the other team's coach was in collusion. Aaron's team was in the lead by six points and the game was in the fourth quarter. My father caught the other coach gesturing to the ref to do something in their favor and my father immediately stormed out of the game enraged. Just a few minutes later my father walked back into the gym with a bat. With the bat in his hand, he walked right over to the other team's coach. At this point, some of the players stopped playing to see what my father was going to do. My mother and I were flabbergasted. She told me to stay put as she dashed over to the other side of the gym to try and stop my father from doing whatever he had planned to do. I could see people focused on the disruption my father had caused. I did not see Aaron on the court and I scanned the floor and spotted him leaving the gym. I could tell he was angry and embarrassed... so was I. I looked back over to my parents. I could barely see my father shouting something at the coach as he put the bat to his face. My mother tried to pull my father away as he swung the bat, but she was unsuccessful. His swing hit one of the players as he pushed my mother out of the way. There was so much chaos! My brother's team was disqualified and Aaron lost all of his potential college scholarships.

My phone rang or at least I thought it was my phone. The ring didn't sound familiar. I glanced over into the passenger seat and there was Dr. Brice's phone. I almost caused an accident pulling the car over to go through his messages. I was hesitant about answering his phone because I did not know who would be on the line. I grabbed his phone anyway and looked to see who was calling. It was a private number. I could not resist the temptation. "Hello?" I answered cautiously.

"Juanita?" Dr. Brice asked.

His voice was mesmerizing. "I could really love this man," I thought to myself.

"Hello, Juanita?" Dr. Brice asked again.

"You left your phone in my car, Kingston." I replied. He laughed after I called him Kingston again and suggested we meet somewhere, so he could get his phone back. Instead, I told him that I would drop his phone off at his office in the morning because I was very tired. I just wanted to get home, take a shower and relax because I could feel a headache emerging. But if I was honest with myself, I really wanted to see him. I wanted him to come in and "talk". I chuckled after thinking about these things.

I heard a woman in the background say, "Dinner's ready."

My ears perked up. "He doesn't wear a ring so I doubt if he's married," I gathered.

He kept insisting we meet somewhere. I guess the woman in the background was not all that important if he felt a great need to come get his phone. "Kingston, I'll drop it off to you tomorrow morning. Good night," I firmly repeated and quickly hung up the phone.

I turned onto my street and pulled up to my home. It was dark. How did I end up being alone? I am twenty-eight and all I have is a few degrees, a great job and a home. All of these material things that I worked so hard to attain still didn't make me happy. I sighed as I just sat in the car and allowed a collection of thoughts to control my feelings. I just pray Harold doesn't stop by tonight because I would let him in so I wouldn't have to be alone.

I finally dragged myself out of the car and walked into my lonely home. Today was really a setback. I wished Grandma Mae were here to help me through this. I wanted to feel safe. I needed her comfort. I opened a new bar of soap and went to take a shower before eating. After I showered, I opened the medicine cabinet to get some aspirin. By this time, I had a full-fledged headache. I shut the medicine cabinet and I caught a glimpse of myself in its mirror. I closed my eyes to avoid thinking of my mother. I took two aspirin and sprawled out on the bed for a few minutes hoping the pain would subside. I began humming one of my mother's favorite songs, *This Little Light of Mine,* which apparently put me to sleep. The doorbell awakened me. I leaped out of bed and fell right to the floor. Splat! I tried to get up but a sharp pain in my ankle made me pause. I sat up for a minute to get myself together. I never slept on the edge of the bed. I wish I had when I was younger then maybe I would not have fallen.

When my father would come into the room and randomly beat us because he was angry, I would be the one who got it the worse. Sometimes, Taylor and I would get into Shanice's bed. I would sleep in the middle to keep my sisters safe. They both wanted to sleep next to me. With me sleeping in the middle seemed to solve that problem.

The doorbell rang again. "Who could this be?" I grumbled as I tried to get off the floor and stand on my injured ankle.

I had on grandma Mae's nightgown. I wish she were here so I can see her wearing it, instead of me. The smell of her is still in it when the fabric softener wears off. Oh, I miss that lady so much.

Someone rang the doorbell for the third time. I was so annoyed. I finally got up but I think I sprained my ankle. It was awfully painful to walk so I limped to open the door only to find Dr. Brice standing on my doorstep. I was embarrassed at my disheveled appearance. Had I known he was going to show up here, I would have put on something more appealing. Maybe a chiffon one-piece lingerie. Whatever it takes... I like how Juanita Brice sounds.

"I told you I would drop your phone off at your office tomorrow morning," I reminded him. The irritation in my voice was evident.

"I tried calling you, but you didn't answer my phone or yours," Dr. Brice replied with a puzzled look on his face.

"My phone is dead. Besides, I told you I would bring it to you tomorrow," I said and then sighed.

"I know, but I need my phone today. My life is on my phone." Dr. Brice responded.

"I'm really tired, Dr. Brice. Let me go get it for you," I answered. I turned around to go get his phone and I fell straight to the floor. "Sure, just pile on the embarrassment why don't you," I thought to myself! I just started crying. I'm mentally and physically tired. I'm embarrassed and I'm emotionally distraught. Dr. Brice rushed to my aid. I tried not to cry but I couldn't hold it in. Maybe I need an antidepressant? Nope... I never took pills and I never will.

Dr. Brice tried to help me up but I resisted. I could not get up because of the pain in my ankle but he didn't know that. The next thing I knew he sat on the floor next to me. I looked into his eyes and then I turned and looked towards the floor. He put his hand on my chin and lifted up my head. He smiled. What I really needed was a hug.

A car had hit my mother one night after picking me up from Grandma Mae's house. Someone hit her while backing out of the parking lot. She pushed me out of the way to protect me from getting hit. I knew she was banged up pretty badly because all I heard was moaning and groaning. I was hysterical. I was screaming and pacing around her. The driver stopped, then put the car in drive and pulled up. An older woman jumped out of another car and ran to my mother's aid. A man with a black, red and navy-blue robe appeared out of nowhere and said he would go in his house and call 911. He ran off. I noticed he didn't have on any shoes. I remember everything as if it had just happened. The older woman kept saying sorry as she tried her best to make sure my mother was at least comfortable until the ambulance arrived. I stood off about six feet away and watched everything. I had stopped crying and moved away from my mother once the driver reached my mother. It was like watching a movie.

"Honey, are you okay?" the driver asked out of concern. I did not or could not answer her. It was as if I was locked into this still scene. Another woman emerged and I could see her walking over towards me.

"Your mother will be okay," she said and then hugged me. It was as though she unlocked my voice. All of the emotions of what had just occurred poured out of me as I felt relief and comfort. I began to cry *uncontrollably. I hugged her tightly as her words gave me faith that my mother was going to make it.*

Dr. Brice asked me if I needed help. Of course I do but I didn't want Dr. Brice's help. I wanted Kingston's help. Okay, yes I said it. I think I would fall for any man at the rate that I'm going.

Dr. Brice softly asked again, "Do you want me to help you up?" With tears running down my face, I shook my head yes. He gently put my arm around his neck and picked me up. Is this a dream? A dream or not, I need to get him out of my house. My breath wasn't the freshest so I swallowed my saliva really hard before I spoke. But before I could say a word, he sat me on my sofa and kissed my forehead, like Grandma Mae used to do. How did he know I needed that too?

"Did you hurt yourself?" Dr. Brice asked as he watched me rub my ankle.

"I think I sprained my ankle when I fell out of bed," I replied.

"How did that happen?" he asked. I was a little embarrassed but I told him that the doorbell startled me when it rang and I fell out of bed. I didn't want to tell him about the beatings as a kid and the whole edge of the bed thing because this topic would come up in one of our sessions.

He picked up his phone from the coffee table and was about to leave. But I didn't want him to leave. I have so many questions to ask him. I didn't know how to ask him because we have more of a doctor patient relationship. I wasn't sure if he would go into some type of rage or not if I asked him about the woman I saw him with today. He walked over to my reading chair, took the leopard print blanket off of and covered me up with it.

"Can I give you a hug?" Dr. Brice politely asked me.

"Yeah, sure," I said nonchalantly as I braced my hand on the sofa seat to get up. He grabbed my hand to help me. He gently wrapped his arms around my waist and brought me close to his muscular body. I was this close to kissing his neck. Oh, my goodness he smells so nice. I didn't want to let him go. I could feel him slowly releasing me after a few seconds so I let go slowly, too, because I did not want to appear desperate. Oh, what the heck! I grabbed him tightly again and whispered in his ear, "Thank you." Dr. Brice continued to hold me for a few more seconds and then he tenderly pulled me away from his body and looked me in the eyes.

"You are welcome, beautiful," he said softly. He then kissed me on my cheek and helped me to sit back on the sofa. I wanted him to force himself on me because my body was yearning for him at that very moment.

"He called me beautiful," I thought as I relished the moment and stored it in my memory.

He kneeled down in front of me and asked, "Can I get you anything before I leave?" I told him no and he took my right hand and held it as he stood up to leave. He let my hand go and the doorbell rang. He looked at me to make sure it was okay to open my door. I gave him the head nod. Dr. Brice opened the door and Taylor looked at him suspiciously. She paused and then looked over at me. I was wiping my eyes. Taylor automatically thought Dr. Brice had done something to me.

"What have you done to my sister?" she screamed accusingly.

Dr. Brice backed up and pleaded with Taylor to relax. She ran over to protect me like I used to do for her when my father would push her around because she took too long to brush her teeth or any other little thing that irritated him.

I assured Taylor that Dr. Brice had done nothing to hurt me. Dr. Brice was caught off guard by Taylor's aggression. I could tell he did not want to be confrontational because he looked back at me before he walked out as if to say, "Clear this up with your sister!" He left without a word. His exit reminded me of Shanice's ex-boyfriend when she told him she might be pregnant.

"That's Dr. Brice?" Taylor inquired in disbelief. "He is hot!" she said excitedly.

"Yes, and I know he's hot," I said with a smile on my face because I agreed with her one thousand percent. Beauty is in the eye of the beholder and we were both beholding how handsome he was.

Taylor said she stopped by to make sure I was okay and to let me know that she would be at the hospital with Aaron in the morning. She said she tried to call me but her call went straight to voicemail. I told her I forgot to charge my phone and detailed how I sprained my ankle.

"Sure your phone was dead," Taylor laughed. "I can see why you didn't answer," she said, implying that I did not want to be disturbed.

"My phone really was dead," I insisted. What do I have to lie for? She gives me grief sometimes but I know there is nothing she wouldn't do for me. Taylor is very understanding and caring. I told her that I would be up to see Aaron sometime tomorrow. She said after she leaves the hospital she would run to the store to pick up some bandages and crutches for me so I can get around. I wouldn't expect anything less from her. Always thinking about what she can do to help.

When we were in grade school there was this girl named Hannah who dressed poorly and smelled like urine all the time. Hannah would wear the same shirt and pants to school at least three times a week. Not only did her clothes smell like urine but they also looked dirty as if they had not been washed all week. When I would see Hannah crying, I knew it was because someone had made fun of her. A lot of the other kids would make fun of her or talk behind her back.

Taylor came home crying over Hannah's situation when she found out that Hannah was homeless and sleeping in the car with her mother and baby brother. Things were really bad for her. Taylor decided to sell her doll clothes that she made by hand to some of the other girls in school. Taylor would use the money to buy Hannah lunch and give her extra food to take home. She even found out what size Hannah and her little brother wore and asked some of the parents in the community if they would donate old clothes so that Hannah and little brother would have nicer clothes. Taylor also stopped most of the bullying of

Hannah by threatening to tell the principal that they were bullying Hannah.

About an hour after Taylor left, the doorbell rang again. My ankle had become even more painful and swollen as I limped to open it. I was surprised to find Dr. Brice standing there again! He had gone to the store; bought bandages and crutches for me. I think he is trying to get a nightcap. He insisted on wrapping my foot and he did it so tenderly. "Dr. Brice?" I said softly.

"Kingston, call me Kingston," Dr. Brice replied. I melted. Does he do this for all his patients? Just thinking about the possibility made me jealous.

Harold was like this in the beginning of our relationship. He would come to my job and surprise me with moon pies, flowers and movie dates during my lunchtime. All of my coworkers were envious of my relationship. He never gave me the opportunity to surprise him. One day, I decided to return the favor and surprise him at this job. I went to the front desk and asked if I could see Harold. "We don't have a Harold here." the receptionist said.

He didn't work there? Maybe I had the wrong place… No, I had the right place.

"We never had anyone named Harold working here,"
she insisted.

She was positive because she's been with the company since its inception. I immediately called Harold and told him I was going to meet him at his job and he told me to come in about twenty minutes because he was in a meeting. I parked my car down the street and out of sight. I waited for him to drive by. Eventually, he came speeding down the street. I waited a couple of minutes and then drove up to meet him as if I was never there. He walked out the front door of the building just like he worked there. I asked him why he lied to me about working at this company when he never had. Harold became very angry. He started yelling and screaming. I told him I "don't do liars" and that I deserved better. As I walked away, he began to plead with me not to leave. I drove off.

I came home later that night to find Harold waiting on my front steps. I asked him politely to leave and he said okay. I turned my back to open my door and he grabbed me by my hair from behind and dragged me into my house. He beat me up that night and stayed at my bedside smoking cigarettes all night to make sure I did not leave or call the police.

After Kingston finished bandaging my ankle, he asked if it was okay for him to stay for a couple of hours. My body said YES, my mind said NO.

"Yes, that would be nice," I said humbly.

We sat quietly for about five minutes before I broke the ice and offered him a cup of coffee, which he graciously made for both of us. I rented a movie from Netflix. We both laughed and talked like we really knew each other. I didn't feel like he was trying to be Dr. Brice. It felt like a date. Doesn't he have to work in the morning? I'm trying to understand what is going on. I was getting ready to ask him why he came back when his phone rang. He looked at the caller ID but didn't answer the call. Who is calling him this late? Was that the older woman whose identity I have yet to know? He leaned back and finished watching the movie. Every now and then he would ask me if I was comfortable. He put ice in a sandwich bag and put my foot on his lap and iced my ankle. Before I could say "no" he was already doing it.

The movie ended. Dr. Brice insisted on ordering pizza. I agreed because I was starving. When the pizza guy came, he paid for it and left. I didn't want him to leave.

I wished all of this was a dream then my sudden confusion would be irrelevant. But it wasn't a dream because I was wide-awake and yearning for his touch. His lips pressed against mine. It was pure torture having him next to me but not being able to feel his touch the way a woman needs to. I desired him to explore every inch of me.

CHAPTER 3

Two and a half weeks have gone by since my brother has been in the hospital. Aaron is making great progress. I spent countless hours at the hospital helping him get back on his feet. He was in bed for six days straight before gaining the strength to walk from the bed to the bathroom without any assistance. Yesterday, the doctor came to Aaron's room and signaled for me to join him in the hallway.

The doctor had the same look on his face that the doctor had the day my father beat Aaron so badly my mother had to call 911. What I do recall is, I was coming home from the library and the ambulance was in front of my home. I was about to run in the house to see what was going on when the EMTs were rushing Aaron out the door on the gurney. I saw my mother frantically crying as she followed them out of the house. The tears were streaming down her face. I went inside to look for Shanice and Taylor. When I found them, they were in the room huddled in the corner crying. I walked toward my parent's room and my father was sitting on the edge of the bed with his head in his hands. I ran back down the hall away from their room, grabbed my sisters and jumped in the car with my mother. Shanice, Taylor and I were petrified as we headed to the hospital. After a few hours at the hospital, the doctor walked into the room with his head down looking at Aaron's file in his hands. The way the doctor looked up from the file then at my mother, I knew something was terribly wrong.

My heart started racing and the familiar feeling of being petrified came over me. I couldn't control the saliva build up in my mouth. I slowly got out of my seat and walked outside of Aaron's room to speak with his doctor. "What could the doctor have found?" I wondered. However, I kept silent as I anticipated some grave news. I kept eye contact as I approached him hoping I could get a read on his facial expression. I took a deep sigh and then I said, "What's up, doc?" He chuckled and I relaxed my shoulders. I exhaled because I thought he was going to tell me that Aaron was going to die and there was nothing else they could do for him.

I received a phone call about six weeks before my father passed away. My mother called me while I was in school getting my Master's. Things were already chaotic because I was at the end of the semester and my dissertation was due.

"Juanita," she would sing as she called my name.

"Hey, Ma, what's up?" I replied.

"Lawrence…" she said sadly and stopped short.

Oh, how I hate to hear his name. I wanted to vomit!

"Your father is dying," she said sadly.

A sense of peace blanketed my mind as if I'd been exonerated from a murder I didn't commit. I was ecstatic but sad at the same time. I wondered how my mother felt. He was all she knew. "What's wrong with him?" I questioned her with hostility. My mother never changed from her soft and warm demeanor.

"He has pancreatic cancer. They're only giving him a couple of months to live," she recounted and sighed deeply. I didn't mumble a word. My mother waited for me to respond. When she realized I had nothing else to say she cleared her throat. "Juanita, are you going to come see him?" she questioned. I could tell that she was extremely emotional and that his sickness had taken its toll on her as well. "Could you answer me?" my mother asked.

She already knew the answer. Why would she put this burden on me? I lived through that violent and sometimes indescribable life. If I look at him, I might kill him before the cancer does. I don't hate anyone but he's very close.

"I can't, Ma," I finally answered.

She hung up on me. My mother stayed with him until the end. Still a dreadful thought.

I barely slept last night. I kept dreaming Aaron had passed away. Much to my relief, the doctor said Aaron was going to live. He really called me into the hall because he wanted to know if Shanice was in a relationship.

"Shanice will be up a little later," I said with a smile and then I suggested he talk to her.

Doctors and cops have the worst work-life-balance schedules. I did not want to be the one connecting my sister with another failed relationship. Even though Shanice wouldn't say it, I know deep down inside she would blame me. If it did work out between the two of them, I could at least say I told him to go for it.

I left the hospital to head home. I needed to take a shower and prepare myself for my therapy appointment.

I haven't seen Dr. Brice since Aaron's hospitalization, but he texted me everyday to make sure I was okay, which was admirable. Every time I picked up the phone to call him or go to a scheduled therapy appointment, I felt as though I was taking time away from Aaron. Taylor, Shanice and I needed to make sure Aaron was getting all of the attention he needed.

I bought a new pair of heels especially for my appointment today. This is the first time I've been able to wear a pair of heels on both feet in over two weeks. Not only do I want to make a statement when I'm in therapy, I want Dr. Brice to fantasize about "knowing" me! I know I'm crossing the lines but I don't care. And I don't think he does either.

I rushed out of the door and to the car, which was parked in the driveway and not in the garage. The automatic door lock was on my front door so there was no need for my keys to be in my hand. I made it to the car and ruffled through my purse only to realize the keys were in my house. I walked back to the front door hoping that it would miraculously be unlocked. No miracles today. Even though I have an extra set of keys in the garage, I can't access them because my car is parked in the driveway and not in the garage. After this episode, I'm really going to get a smart home security system installed where I can unlock my door with my phone.

I was already running late for my appointment but now there's no way I'm going to be able to make it. I wasn't ready to miss my appointment because I miss seeing Dr. Brice... plus I was looking extra tempting today. I texted Taylor 911 but it only works if she gets the message and comes to help me. It's been at least five minutes and I haven't heard back from her yet. Shanice can't help me either because she's at an offsite training more than two hours away.

I decided to call Dr. Brice's office to cancel today's appointment and reschedule for the following week. After rescheduling my appointment I booked a rideshare so I could go up to the hospital while I waited for Taylor to get back to me.

Twelve minutes later, I am still waiting for my ride. I thought about walking to the hospital, which was a little over a mile away. But I had on a new pair of black and white pumps and I wasn't about to see if they would hold up for an hour straight without my feet aching.

I was about to call an Uber, which I should've done in the first place when my phone rang. The display read "private caller". Who could this be? "Hello?" I answered the phone. There was complete silence. "Who is this?" I questioned the caller again.

"Juanita," said Dr. Brice.

He's going to want to know why I'm missing my appointment. "What do I say?" I thought to myself. Wait a minute, I'm grown and I don't have to explain anything!

"Is everything okay, Juanita?" Dr. Brice asked.

"Yeah, I just locked myself out of my car and house." I blurted out.

"Where are you?" he asked. I told him I was home and about to call an Uber.

"I'm coming over right now!" he exclaimed. I began to stutter because that's not what I expected, but it was definitely what I wanted.

"It's okay, Dr. Brice. I can arrange a ride," I told him. However, he insisted I wait for him to pick me up.

I can still feel a little pain in my ankle since the sprain so I sat on the stairs and fifteen minutes later Dr. Brice pulled up.

"Oh My Goodness!" I said when he got out of the car. He took my breath away. He had on a maroon vest with a blue, white, and maroon dress shirt. A pretty paisley tie complimented his entire outfit. His dark blue dress pants were fitted enough to see his bulge. I wasn't trying to look but I couldn't help it. By the time I inspected his wing tip shoes he reached for my hand. Oh my gosh he's such a gentle man, I mean a gentleman. He's both. Oh, who am I kidding... I am falling for him with every encounter.

He opened his car door and waited for me to get in. "Ah," I exhaled. His car was filled with a soft vanilla and spice aroma. Dr. Brice is wearing new cologne today too. I wonder if he wore it just for me? I am sure he did and I will not accept any other reasoning.

"Don't you have more clients today?" I asked before he closed my door.

"You were my last client today," he replied. He then licked his already moist lips.

"I could have kept my appointment," I thought. "You didn't have to come get me you know?" I said softly.

"I know," he said and then paused. "I wanted to see you today."

I blushed. My body was screaming, "TAKE ME, I'M ALL YOURS"!

"Look at me," he requested.

I turned and looked at him. He ran his hand down my back. He then leaned over and kissed me. What should I do? It was just a peck but I read between the lines. There's more to come! He didn't apologize this time. I just kept silent as the lines became blurred yet obvious. I didn't want whatever this was going to be, to become more convoluted than it already was. Should I just be forward? I'm not just looking for a play date. I want a husband. I refuse to settle for just being with someone. I know I need to get my mental situation under control; however, I still deserve to be with this man. I mean a man that is all mine.

He closed my car door and then got into the driver's seat. "You look beautiful every time I see you," he said with a smile after he turned the music down.

"Thank you," I replied as my tongue grazed my top lip.

I really wanted to express how gorgeous and well dressed he always looks, but I was taught not to extend a compliment directly after one has been given. I was so tempted to return the compliment, as I really wanted him to know how I saw him.

Grandma Mae and I were at the farmers market one summer. An older gentleman walked by us, stopped and commented on how beautiful she was. She said thank you and we carried on. He was very handsome. I was young but I wasn't blind. I asked Grandma Mae how come she didn't tell him he was cute? Grandma Mae said thank you was enough. If she had complimented him after he extended one then it wouldn't be as genuine. I said okay then we bought some fruit. I didn't know exactly what she meant then but now I do. She was the balance to my sanity.

He kept gawking at my shoes. I know he loved them because I did. Shame on me! I was trying to entice him. I can't blame him for being distracted. But I haven't felt this good about myself in a long time. I needed this feeling back in my life.

Dr. Brice inhaled and then exhaled deeply. "Where would you like to go?" he asked. I didn't want to go to the hospital. I just wanted to stay in his company forever.

"Would you still like to have your session?" Dr. Brice asked.

I don't think we could see each other and he continues as my therapist; although, I wouldn't mind that.

"I know this is complicated so I'll give you a choice," he stated.

"What's the choice, Kingston?" I inquired.

"We can explore us or I can continue to be your therapist," he replied.

I don't want to choose. Why does this have to be so difficult? Why would he want to hook up with me knowing the things he knows about me? I came to him for help and I still needed help. I don't think he is trying to take advantage of my vulnerability, but I am faced with a dilemma. I want to know all about him. I need to know more.

I turned my head toward the street and I saw Harold's car pulling up to my house. I had never told Dr. Brice about Harold. I mean absolutely nothing. Not about my previous abusive relationship or him even stopping by every now and then.

"Why today, Harold? You better not mess this up for me or you'll never see me again," I angrily thought to myself. I could feel my nose flaring, as I was instantly stricken with the aggravation of him showing up. Whenever Harold came over that meant he needed something. This was not a good time for him to need something. How would he react seeing me in the car with Dr. Brice? I still don't know what Harold does for work. After he beat me up that day I never questioned where he got his money. He usually wants money, sex or somewhere to lay his head. It's my fault he's here because I never closed that door. I always gave in to him. The years of abuse kept me unsure of my ability to be loved properly.

I should have ended it when I first left him but every time I opened the door and let him in, it meant there was still a possibility. The last time Harold came over he was crying because he had lost his job and was going to be evicted if he didn't come up with his lease payment. He needed to borrow a few thousand dollars until his unemployment commenced. He knew I made a lot of money so I gave him four thousand dollars and sent him on his way. That was the last time I saw him and that was months ago. What could he need now? Perhaps he was coming to pay me back. Who am I fooling? I know better than to think that.

Dr. Brice didn't notice Harold but Harold saw Dr. Brice reach over to kiss me again. Harold jumped out of his car and headed towards us. I quickly pushed Dr. Brice away from me. Harold is very possessive and jealous; therefore, I was expecting the worst.

"What's going on?" Harold yelled as he approached Dr. Brice's car.

He ran over to the passenger door and yanked it open. I was terrified.

"Get out of the car!" Harold screamed at me.

Dr. Brice jumped out the car as Harold grabbed my arm trying to pull me out. I was afraid because I didn't know how aggressive Harold was going to get. All of a sudden Harold yanked me out of the car and twisted my arm. Dr. Brice ran over and punched Harold in the face. Harold swung back at Dr. Brice but missed and fell into my newly planted flowerbed. Dr. Brice began hitting Harold uncontrollably. Then Dr. Brice suddenly stopped and got back on his feet with his fists balled up.

Harold was barely moving. I wanted to run to Dr. Brice's rescue but I didn't. Instead I needed to call the police but I couldn't find my phone so I dumped everything out of my pocketbook desperately hunting for it. It took forever to find my phone. I dialed 911 and could barely articulate my words before the operator calmed me down and obtained the needed information to send the police.

I was extremely nervous. Dr. Brice noticed I was shaking and immediately stepped away from being on guard with Harold and attended to me. "Are you okay?" Dr. Brice asked. I shook my head no and started crying. He held me like my mother used to hold me when she knew I was scared. While he consoled me, Dr. Brice kept a watchful eye on Harold. I felt his heart racing or was it mine?

Harold tried to get up but kept stumbling. Dr. Brice let me go so he could help Harold up but Harold resisted his help. I heard the police sirens. A sigh of relief came over me. Now I'm afraid that Harold will show up at my house and threaten my life after this ordeal.

The police arrived and arrested Harold for assault. Thank God the neighbors were able to corroborate my side of the story or Harold would've gotten away. The officer suggested that I file a restraining order against him. I agreed.

I was still a little shaken up. Dr. Brice made sure I sat back in the car and was calm before we drove off heading to the hospital. We didn't say much to each other on the way there.

I wondered what was going through his mind and what kind of questions he might ask me about Harold.

"Are you okay?" he asked.

"We can't see each other," I blurted out.

"What do you mean?" he asked.

I told him that everything was messy and this is not how I wanted to start off a relationship.

"I understand," he said calmly as he kept his eyes on the road.

How strong were his feelings toward me? Did he really want to be in a relationship with me or did he really want to satisfy his sexual appetite? Was being with me a game?

We finally made it to the hospital. I unbuckled my seatbelt and was about to get out.

"I will see you next week Ms. Winfield," he said as I exited the car.

I could tell Dr. Brice was upset, but I think things would be better if he remained my therapist.

CHAPTER 4

I walked into Aaron's room only to discover someone else in his assigned bed. I rushed to the nurses' station to inquire where my brother was transferred. They stated that he had discharged himself against medical advice.

"He wasn't well!" I exclaimed. They stated that he was well enough to leave and they couldn't stop him. I was livid! I stood in the middle of the hospital corridor and looked around. Now what? I didn't even have time to spend with him while he was sober. I wanted to recapture some of the time we lost in the past three years. I put my hand on my heart and I fought back the tears. I still hadn't heard from Taylor. So much for the 911 text. Now, what do I do because I don't have a ride home? Taylor hasn't called me and our brother is missing in action. I started walking. I might as well grab a cup of coffee then go down to the waiting room until I heard from Taylor.

Besides being frustrated about Aaron's premature release, I couldn't stop thinking about Dr. Brice. I think the choice I made was best. What good would I be to him? I'm broken. I'm really trying to convince myself that it wouldn't work.

I made my way down to the hospital café. I figure I should get comfortable because I don't know how long I'm going to be here waiting for Taylor to come get me. I must've stood in front of the coffee station for about ten minutes. They had four unfamiliar coffee selections. I didn't know what to choose.

"Try the vanilla butter crisp, it's really good," a gentleman said,

I immediately turned around to see who was offering their advice. One eyebrow went up. I slipped and pleasantly said, "Mmmm!" I can't believe I just verbalized what I was thinking in front of this complete stranger. "Just because you recommended it, I'll try it," I replied to cover up my embarrassment.

"You won't be disappointed," he insisted.

"We'll see," I replied and snickered.

"Hi, I'm Gabriel," he said.

"Juanita," I said and smiled.

I thanked him and fixed my coffee. It smelled so good... almost as good as Gabriel looked. I headed to the cash register. The cashier told me that Gabriel had already paid for my coffee. I turned around to see where he went so I could thank him but I didn't see him. I wish he hadn't disappeared because I really wanted to look at him one more time. There's really nothing wrong with looking when you're single. I generously tipped the cashier and walked off.

After church one Sunday, my mother, Shanice, Taylor, Aaron and I stopped home to pick up my father so we all could go out for ice cream. We left church so excited. As a family, we headed to the "Big Ice" ice cream shop. We would go there two to three times during the summer. It was one of my favorite places to go. My mother ordered our favorite ice cream with toppings while my dad went to find us seats. Everything was going well. Once we found our seats my father went up to help my mother. My father handed the cashier money to pay for our treats. The cashier refused his money and told my father that the guy before us had already paid for it. My father asked if the person was still in the shop and the cashier pointed to the man sitting three tables away from us enjoying his ice cream. My mother picked up the tray of ice cream so she could bring it over to our table when my father turned to her and asked her if she knew the guy or why he bought our food. My mother said no with a confused look on her face.

"Liar!" my dad exclaimed! He then knocked the tray of ice cream out of my mother's hands. "Now pick it up seeing you like picking up men!" my father said

sarcastically. My father turned away from my mother and walked over to the man that paid for our food. He pushed the man over in his chair and threw the money at the man. The man looked confused. My father told him not to pay for a married woman's food again.

The man shouted, "I didn't pay for anybody's food!"

Come to find out, the cashier made a mistake. We didn't eat ice cream that day. My father was notorious for ruining family time.

I walked down the corridor heading to the general waiting room and there was Gabriel conversing with a doctor. He sipped his coffee and looked away from the doctor. We locked eyes and he smiled at me. He took his hand out of his pocket and held up his index finger signaling me to wait a minute.

You can tell he was rushing through his conversation because he was quickly inching away from the doctor as he was talking. I tried to occupy myself by looking at some of the artwork hanging on the wall but I couldn't help but sneak peeks of Gabriel. I wondered if he noticed me watching him. I can imagine him calling my name with his full set of lips, white teeth and raspy voice. I replayed the brief encounter we had in my mind about six times in the last couple of minutes.

Gabriel walked over to me after he finished talking to the doctor. He was smiling and rubbing his hands together like he had something to tell me.

"I really want to thank you for paying for my coffee," I said with a smile.

"How did you like it?" he asked.

"I love it!' I answered and took another sip. "I owe you one."

"You have a minute?" Gabriel asked.

"I do," I replied blushing.

He suggested that if I finished my coffee with him, we would be even. I gladly accepted because I had nothing else to do but wait. We laughed as he told me some funny things that had happened to him in college. Our conversation was wild but not awkwardly personal. He also told me that he's a pharmaceutical sales executive and that he restores classic cars in his spare time. I know a lot about classic cars because my neighbor collected classic models. Gabriel was quite impressed at how much I knew about cars. I think it turned him on because he couldn't stop biting his bottom lip as I named a dozen names and years of Chevy and Ford classics. I think I enjoyed getting him aroused more than he enjoyed my intellect on that subject. After about an hour, Gabriel had to go and before he walked off, he gently kissed my hand. It was good to get my mind off of everything for a change.

As I waited for Taylor or Shanice to call me, I basked in the conversation I just had with Gabriel. My thoughts were playing ping-pong between Dr. Brice and Gabriel.

Taylor finally replied to my 911 text and said she was on her way to pick me up from the hospital. She was furious after I told her that the hospital released Aaron. I know Aaron is a man and can make decisions for himself; however, I don't think he was well enough to leave. We decided to ride around looking for Aaron to no avail. After three hours, we gave up searching for him in hopes he would turn up at Taylor's house by nightfall. I really wanted to talk to Taylor about Dr. Brice but I didn't want what she thought to crush any feelings I had towards him. She did ask a few questions about him but I only disclosed what I wanted her to know.

Taylor gave me a giant hug and relaxed her body in my arms. I know she needed me. I'm also certain that things from our past have surfaced but she wasn't ready to talk about "it" either. We are never really ready to talk about "it". I suggested she check in with me tomorrow or call me as soon as she hears from Aaron.

Taylor's fiancé, Eric, is really genuine and engaging. They've been seeing each other for several years now. I know she agreed to their engagement just to appease Eric. Taylor isn't ready. She suggested I go see a therapist and I sure hope she's practicing what she's preaching. I don't know if we don't talk about our personal lives to one another because of our father but whatever the unknown reason is we surely adhered to it. Taylor doesn't know that I talk to Eric's sister, Faryn, every now and again. The last time I saw Faryn she pleaded with me to talk to Taylor. In confidence, Eric shared with Faryn that he doesn't know what's wrong with Taylor. He says they get along great but she won't agree on a wedding date. He wants them to purchase a house together, but she doesn't want to talk about it with him. I politely told Faryn that I can't get in between their situation and neither should she. If Taylor found out that Eric even mentioned their personal business with anyone, Taylor would leave him. That's just how Taylor is, no nonsense. I asked Taylor when her wedding date was. She turned to me and said, and I quote, "When I set it, you'll know." I could hear my father in her tone and see him in her eyes. I knew then she wanted me to stay out of her business. My father's character carried over in our lives in bits and pieces. I think Taylor is afraid her marriage would be like our parents.

Taylor said okay and left after she watched me go into the house. I looked back to wave bye when I noticed there was an unfamiliar car parked a few houses down with its parking lights on.

It was good to finally be home but I felt unsafe. I closed the door and made sure every window and door was locked just in case Harold showed up. I didn't want to live in fear anymore but I don't have someone here with me that will protect me. I will go to the courthouse and file a restraining order against Harold tomorrow.

I plopped down on my sofa and took off my heels. I grabbed my phone to check my messages. I had no messages. I tossed my phone back in my purse and sat back. My thoughts went right to Gabriel. He was very attractive, had a great sense of humor and appeared to be financially stable. "Who am I kidding?" I mumbled to myself. He's not my type. I took a deep sigh as I stretched out on my sofa. I rested my head back on the sofa's arm and stared at the ceiling. I closed my eyes and drifted into a review of the day's events. Just a few hours ago I told Dr. Brice that he and I wouldn't work as a couple and now I'm home alone fantasizing about

Gabriel. I didn't even ask Gabriel if he was in a relationship because I really didn't want to know. That would've ruined the superficial attraction I had towards him.

I tried to watch television but it watched me. I finally got up from the sofa, went into my room to get undressed and took a shower. I walked by my beautifully, flowered framed, wall mirror and stopped in front of it. I looked at myself naked and wondered what Dr. Brice would think of my body. How would he touch me? How would he hold me? After a few moments in deep thought I walked in the bathroom and got in the shower. I stood directly under the showerhead and let the waterfall off the curves of my body. I pressed against the wall and put my head underneath the steady stream of water for a few minutes before washing my body. I finally got out of the shower and dried myself off. I felt so refreshed and relaxed. I tied my hair up in the towel so I didn't have to blow dry it. I slipped on a red, satin, two-piece, lace lingerie and climbed into bed. The next thing I knew it was morning. I had nothing to do. No one to see and nowhere to go so I just stayed in bed. My phone rang but I couldn't find it. It was buried in my pocket book. When I finally dug it out, I had missed the call. It was from a private number. This had to be Dr. Brice. Should I call him back?

I was able to get Dr. Brice's cell phone number when he left his phone in my car. What if that wasn't him that called me?

Was he thinking about me? If that was him, then what could he possibly want? I decided not to call Dr. Brice. Instead, I chose to just lie in the bed and watch some infomercials. I saw this beautiful Benrus vintage 14k gold watch but I wasn't in the market to purchase a watch. They must've talked about that watch for over a half an hour before I gave in and decided to purchase it. I reached for my pocketbook to get my wallet out but it wasn't in there. I knew I had my wallet at the hospital but then again, I couldn't be sure because Gabriel paid for my coffee so I didn't even have to go in my pocketbook to get it. Did someone steal my wallet? I was in a complete panic. I looked in my car for it but it wasn't there. I was sure it was in my pocket book, I think. I searched all over the house but it was still nowhere to be found.

My head began to hurt trying to figure out where my wallet was so I sat and thought about the last time I actually used it. Well, the last time I had it was at the Chinese restaurant two days ago. Well no. Shanice paid for that. I was getting very nervous because my life is in my wallet. I was about to cancel my credit cards and then I remembered dumping my stuff out in Dr. Brice's car looking for my cell phone to call the police on Harold.

I hope he doesn't think I left my wallet in his car on purpose. I'm not even sure if it's in his car. I hesitated before calling him but I needed to find my wallet.

"Hello," Dr. Brice answered.

"It...it...it... it's Juanita, Dr. Brice," I replied. Why was I stammering? I heard the pitch in his voice change. He sounded excited. Thank God he couldn't see my face because I was blushing.

"Juanita, is everything okay?" he asked. I had butterflies in my stomach.

"Did I leave my wallet in your car?" I asked.

"I didn't notice but let me go check," he said as I heard him leave the phone. I was hoping it was in there for a few reasons. One is that I need my identification. The other two would be the hassle of cancelling all of my credit cards and getting a new identification, which is a daunting process.

A few minutes later Dr. Brice returned to the phone. "Are you still there, Juanita?" he asked.

"Yes, I'm here," I answered patiently, waiting for him to let me know if he had found my wallet or not.

"I found it. It was under the passenger seat," he excitedly confirmed.

"What a relief," I said as I placed my hand on my heart.

I'm not going to see Dr. Brice for another five days and I need my wallet. Should I go get it or should I ask him to drop it off this afternoon? I opened my mouth to speak, but before

I could utter another word Dr. Brice said, "I will leave it with my secretary if you need it by five today." I was speechless.

"Are you still there?" he asked.

"Of course I'm still here. I've been here waiting for you to make some moves on me and whisper things in my ears that would be censored if you were to say them out loud!" I screamed silently. I cleared my throat and pulled my hair back. It took a second for me to pull it together before I replied because I honestly thought he really wanted to see me. "Okay, I'll pick it up from your office before five," I responded nonchalantly. I guess he didn't want to see me. In disappointment, I hung up the phone. Why would I expect him to bring me my wallet or even want to see me when yesterday I told him that it would be best if he were "JUST" my therapist?

"I might as well get up and get dressed, "I mumbled to myself. I figured I would go to the lake and read a book after I picked up my wallet.

I grabbed some snacks, *Family of Lies* novel by Mary Monroe and I headed out of the house. I made sure I had my keys this time.

I walked into Dr. Brice's office building and Diane gave me the thumbs up to go up to Dr. Brice's office. I got on the elevator and just as the door was about to close I saw a well-dressed, older lady scurrying to catch it. I stopped the door from closing. She smiled as she entered the elevator. She had beautiful silky, silver hair and flawless skin. Whatever products she is using illuminated her skin.

I immediately thought about Grandma Mae's hair and skin. Maybe it was the water from their era. Grandma Mae used to let me comb her long, silky white hair all the time before the tragic fire. I was only five. I can't remember much from that night when her apartment caught on fire. What I do remember was the apartment fire alarm going off and that the apartment being very hot. I still have a scar on my arm as a reminder.

Grandma Mae told me that she went into the kitchen to check on the stew because it smelled like it was burning. She didn't realize the dishtowel was too close to the stove and had caught on fire. She tried to distinguish it but the fire had already spread. She couldn't put it out. In an effort to call 911, Grandma Mae left the kitchen to grab me to escape the fire that was building in her apartment. She rushed into the living room where I was. She tripped on my toys that were left on the floor. She tried to push me out of the way so she wouldn't fall on me but my arm grazed the coffee table that left this nasty cut, which needed sixteen stitches to close up. Grandma Mae hit her head on the end of the coffee table and was knocked unconscious.

The neighbor said I was screaming, "Get up G-Mae, get up!" to her over and over. I wanted to remember so badly but I couldn't for the life of me.

"Are you okay?" the older lady asked softly.

I pulled up my sleeve and rubbed my hand across the scar. As the tears flowed from my eyes, I shook my head yes. The older lady went into her black clutch purse and pulled out a beautiful vintage Rhode Island embroidered Franshaw Madeira handkerchief from the fifties. It was just like the one Grandma Mae had. I couldn't believe it. I felt an overwhelming sense of comfort. She handed it to me and said, "You can have it." How did she know Grandma Mae had one of those? I didn't even want to get it wet but it would've probably insulted her.

"Thank you," I whispered as I tried to fight back more tears.

Before she exited the elevator, she hugged me like grandma Mae used to do. It felt so real. Alone in the elevator again, I closed my eyes tightly so I could cherish the encounter. I patted my eyes dry, and fixed my blouse before I reached Dr. Brice's floor.

The elevator chimed once we were on the 14th floor. The door opened to an empty waiting area. I got off the elevator and Maureen appeared from the back and greeted me with a beautiful smile and a blissful "Hello". She then excitedly embraced me. I was caught off guard at first, but then I was happy to reciprocate the gesture, as this was the first time she had ever hugged me. Maureen asked me to wait while she went to her desk to retrieve my wallet. While I waited, I noticed Dr. Brice's door was closed. I really wanted to knock on his office door but I convinced myself not to. Maureen handed me my wallet and I headed back to the elevator. I heard talking in the background so I turned around towards Dr. Brice's office and the older woman I saw him arguing with over a week ago was exiting his office. She appeared to be crying. Dr. Brice came out right after her so I quickly turned towards the elevator and put my phone to my ear as if to be conversing with someone. The older woman walked over to the elevator. She looked at me and tried to form a legitimate smile but I knew she was just being cordial. I smiled back as I pretended to be talking on the phone.

I heard Dr. Brice clear his throat and then ask Maureen if I had picked up my wallet. Maureen tried to whisper to him and probably motioned to him that I was waiting at the elevator. I acted as if I didn't hear them conversing by talking to "NO ONE" on the other end of my phone.

The elevator chimed and the door opened. I pretended to hang up my phone as I signaled to the older woman to get on the elevator first and then I felt his hand touch mine. I froze.

"Juanita, do you have a minute?" he asked. I shook my head yes and squeezed his hand tightly. The older woman stepped onto the elevator and then glared at us as the elevator door closed. I couldn't turn and look at him just yet. I didn't know what I wanted. I needed him as my therapist. I needed him as my man but I'm still not sure what to do. He smells so good. I wanted to turn around and rip his shirt off with my bare teeth. With my lips pursed together, I quietly exhaled. Suddenly, I felt his warm breath on my neck. The chase really has me excited. Imagining all of the things he could do to me. Every single touch from him makes me feel erotic.

"I need a minute," I whispered.

"Take as long as you need," he replied. "Is everything okay?"

"Yes, I just need a minute," I answered him as I released his hand. We both just stood there until I was ready to face him. I was very curious as to who the older woman was but instead of letting my curiosity get the best of me, I took a deep breath and then turned around and faced him.

"Thanks," I said. We were less than a foot away from each other. I felt boxed in. "He's at work," I thought to myself so I took a step back.

"Thanks for what?" Dr. Brice asked.

"For finding my wallet," I replied.

He smiled and stared into my eyes as if he was waiting for more but that's all I had to say. Well, not really, but it was all I was going to say unless he asked me another question.

I peeked over Dr. Brice's shoulder. I noticed Maureen smiling at me and she made me smile. He quickly turned around and caught Maureen smiling. Dr. Brice relaxed his shoulders and asked me if I would come into his office for a quick second. I agreed. As he passed Maureen, he told her she could go home early. Maureen immediately opened her desk drawer and pulled out her purse as if it were her last day.

As soon as I walked into his office, I noticed that it had been redecorated. He had a flair for appealing decor.

I sat on the sofa and he sat next to me. He didn't leave any space between us. Our legs were touching and it was making my nipples erect. I was hoping he didn't notice. I began feeling a little nervous because I didn't know what to expect. What does he want to talk to me about? I thought about getting up but why would I do that? Maybe now he'll tell me a little about himself since this was, technically, not one of my therapy sessions.

"I'm sorry, would you like something to drink?" he asked as he got up.

"No, thank you," I answered.

When he got up, he turned and looked at me. I noticed him looking down at my breasts. He looked back at me and licked his lips.

"Are you sure I can't get you anything?" he asked as he slowly glanced back at my breasts.

If only he knew what I was thinking about him. He walked over to his phone that was sitting on his desk and put on some music. He turned it down low then he turned to me to make sure I didn't show any signs of disapproval of his choice of music. Was he trying to push up on me? I watched his every move. He got a bottle of water from his portable glass door refrigerator, took a sip then closed the bottle. He walked back over to me but I turned away so he could enjoy my body responding to his presence without him having to act as if he wasn't laying his eyes on me. He sat next to me but it appeared as though he was even closer this time. I turned my head to face him.

"I really like jazz," he stated enthusiastically.

"I do as well." I concurred.

I didn't want to stop him from talking so I didn't tell him how much I "really" liked jazz, too. I just smiled and said, "REALLY" as he listed a few of his favorite jazz artists and songs. I asked about one of his all-time favorite singers in any genre.

"Undoubtedly, Luther Vandross." he said.

I ran my fingers through my hair and agreed that Luther was in the top ten of my all-time impactful and soulful singers too. Dr. Brice got up again and changed Duke Ellington's song, the *A Train* to Luther Vandross' *Going in Circles.*

He started to sing with the music so I joined in and sang along with him. I couldn't help myself. I hope he wasn't trying to give hints by playing that particular song. As soon as the song ended, we both laughed and I reached over and zealously kissed him. I didn't even realize what I was doing until I was already in motion. We kissed but it was different this time. It's what we both wanted. I'm a grown woman but I knew that if we didn't get to know each other first that whatever was going to happen wouldn't last. Our lips separated as he slid his tongue back in his mouth.

Dr. Brice moved his hands to my lower waist, looked me in my eyes and said, "From the moment you walked into my office I knew you were the one."

I chuckled inside. What? Does he think I just tripped and bumped my head? He could be telling the truth but only he and God knows.

"I ride by your house every day," he stated.

"He's good." I thought to myself.

I'm the one? Does he think I'm that naïve? Why do I have to over analyze every single thing? I had to concentrate because I needed to be aware of everything he was saying. He said everything any woman wanted to hear. Did I just hear him say he loved me? Nah, it was just my imagination running away with me.

"I'm not ready for a relationship." I blurted out.

Dr. Brice removed his hands from my waist. "One day at a time," he replied in a calm manner.

I shook my head yes and then rested my head in his lap while my legs hung over the side of his sofa. I think Dr. Brice knows that I want to be with him badly. He stroked my hair as we listened to the music in silence. I wondered what he was thinking. Every time I try to push him away from me, I'm drawn closer. He turned the music off.

"Do you have anywhere to go?" he asked.

"No," I said. If I say yes then I'll be lying.

"Would you like to watch a movie?" he inquired.

"Sure," I said with certainty.

He got up and grabbed my hand. I stood up and we were face to face. His lips were about six inches from mine. His lips slowly formed a smile. I grazed my top lip with my tongue and raised my left eyebrow. There were so many things I wanted him to do to me. I wore a green silk blouse that buttoned down from the back. He could unbutton it button by button and massage my body with his soft lips beginning at the nape of my neck all the way down to my blouse's seam. Then he could caress my breasts from behind as he lays his head in the pit of shoulder blades.

Instead, he turned and walked in a different direction while still holding my hand. He was bringing me into another room. I was very intrigued. I didn't know there was another room. Once I saw the shelf move and that there was another room, I was a little apprehensive. I slowly pulled my hand away from his hand and firmly stood at the doorway.

"He could kill me and no one would ever know," I thought. I watched him enter into this private room and waved for me to join him. Slowly and cautiously, I entered a room that was almost the same size as his office. My eyes scanned the walls and I caught a whiff of jasmine as it filled the air. The aroma wasn't overwhelming but enough to alleviate the stress and anxiety that I had once I realized he had a hiding place.

Did he choose this scent on purpose? Jasmine is known to help the body to unwind plus it's a natural aphrodisiac.

The walls were covered with artwork of artists I didn't recognize. My knowledge of art wasn't vast; however, I was pretty familiar with Inuit, Maritime, 17th Century, Harlem Renaissance and art by Jacob Lawrence; a 20th century artist. It's as if every piece had been carefully selected and meticulously placed on the wall. There were contemporary themes of architecture drawn in pencil and others painted in watercolor. I also saw a few pieces of Middle Eastern art. I'm not sure of any of the artists but they were beautiful and fascinating. There was a rust colored fabric sectional in the middle of the room with two navy blue leather chairs flanking it. As I continued to look around the room, I was caught off guard by the sound of a projector screen scaling down the back wall. I turned around and looked up at this beautiful colorful, striped wooden valance that hid the screen. Dr. Brice held a remote in his hand as I glanced over to see what he was up to. He pressed a button on the remote and the blinds automatically closed. Oh, how I really like a smart home, a smart office and definitely a smart man... a man after my own heart. He really has good taste. As the blinds closed, a dim light slowly brightened up the darkening room. The ambiance was perfect... soft and peaceful.

Dr. Brice called out a list of movie genres and titles we could watch. After about ten minutes, we finally chose a movie we both would enjoy together.

We watched "Message in A Bottle" and I cried again. I've seen this movie at least seven times and it still pulls at my heart. Throughout the movie, I tried to hold back the tears and would wipe one away one at a time as I pretended to move my hair from my face. By the end of the movie, I could no longer hide my feelings and sobbed when Kevin Costner's boat capsized. I knew what was coming but my emotions hadn't gotten the memo.

"Are you crying?" Dr. Brice asked and then started laughing.

I turned to him slightly embarrassed and said, "Are you making fun of me?

He chuckled and said, "Of course I am."

I took the sofa pillow and hit him.

"Ouch!" he shouted.

I looked up and he was holding one hand over his eye. I know I caught him off guard with the pillow hit but I didn't think his reflexes were that slow. I peeled his hand away from his face and he put his head down. "It couldn't be that bad," I thought to myself. I was about to say something when all of sudden I got a pillow to the face and then it was on... PILLOW FIGHT!!! I can't believe he tricked me like that. While trying to dodge my pillow attack, he bumped into the arm of the sofa and fell on the floor. I figured I would be the better one and help him up. I reached my hand out to call a truce and he grabbed my hand and pulled me on top of him. He was aroused and so was I. This was totally unexpected. Where do we go from here? We could have sex and then what? "Kingston," I whispered.

"Yes," he responded while slightly squinting his eyes.

"We can't do this." I said as I found myself getting drawn into him.

"We can..." he answered, holding back.

I knew it was time to exit stage left because the more I'm around him the cloudier my judgment gets. I gently removed his hands from around my waist and got up. I fixed my blouse and pulled my hair back.

"Do you have to go now?" He asked.

"No, but yes, Kingston," I said as I pulled my hair back again and away from my face. He stayed on the floor but sat up and put both of his hands on his knees. I really don't care what he does just being around him stimulates me. I stood in front of him. I wanted him to see me out but he stayed put.

I had not noticed how beautiful and detailed the Persian rug was. It was at least an inch thick and I figure it cost well over eight thousand dollars. It didn't nap up like a typical oriental rug would like the ones you would purchase from a local discount store.

"Are you going to see me out?" I asked.

"Of course," he answered back and got up from the floor.

Dr. Brice walked me to Maureen's desk. "Can we do this again?" he asked.

"Yes... soon," I answered. That put an immediate smile on his face and he then passionately hugged me and slid his hands down to the top of my butt. Our hips met.

"I had a really good time with you," he whispered in my ear.

I blushed like a high school girl getting asked to the prom by the football captain. I gently released him, but he kept his hands around me sealing us together.

"You could let me go now," I uttered. Dr. Brice reluctantly relinquished his grip.

I walked over to the elevator and pressed the button. It opened instantly. I walked in the elevator and he watched me until the door closed. Once the door closed, I deeply exhaled. A flood of emotions brought tears to my eyes. I was battling with the thought of Dr. Brice moving on if I don't give in soon. Would he discontinue his professional services as well because it would make things complicated for the both of us?

The elevator door opened to the building's lobby. Diane was watching the wall clock like a hawk preying on a rabbit. Her eyes quickly moved from the wall to the elevator area as she noticed me. I waved bye to her and she returned the hand gesture with a smile as she simultaneously took the sign-in kiosk tablet from the receptionist counter. Once I reached the building's front door to exit, I stopped and paused.

"Do I turn back around and let Dr. Brice have his way with me?" I pondered. But I stuck to my guns and headed out of the door to the parking lot and I got into my car. I sat all the way back into the seat, pushed my head back on the headrest in conflict with my feelings. "You should've gone back," I uttered in frustration after gripping the steering wheel tightly. "So much for eating my snacks and reading a book down at the lake," I murmured.

I cranked up the car and drove off. I grabbed the snacks from my bag and drove around looking for Aaron. I stopped at every spot I thought he might be. I even went back to the areas Taylor and I had already been over the past few weeks. I ran into two people who had seen him and said that he looked really bad. I was very worried. I continued to drive around for another hour or so but as night fell I ended my search for him.

I pulled into my garage and waited for the door to close before I unlocked my car doors to get out. I reached over to grab my purse and my cell phone rang. I was hoping it was Dr. Brice. I picked up the phone but it was Taylor. "What could she want?" I wondered.

"Juanita," Taylor shouted.

"Is everything okay?" I asked.

"Aaron is in the hospital again!" she cried out in pandemonium.

"What?" I exclaimed. "What happened? I was just riding around town looking for him." I immediately felt uneasiness in the pit of my stomach.

Just then Taylor screamed, "Nooooo!" and her phone clattered to the floor.

My eyes filled with tears, afraid to hear what had happened but needing to know. "Where are you, Taylor? I asked. What I was assuming I didn't want to be true. Taylor's voice instantly became distant. I could hear her weeping in the background. I've only heard my sister scream like this once before.

Grandma Mae had been sick for a while but on this particular day she was really sick. I had just gotten the consultant job with Holland Technologies and as I was about to leave for work that morning, I heard Grandma Mae moaning. I walked to her room and she was sitting in her chair crying. She would normally be up watching TV but not this day. I helped her get into bed because she looked extremely tired. She could barely walk. The thought of her being in such pain and agony made me want to cry. I waited until I got in my car to cry because I didn't want her to see me not being strong for her. I didn't want to leave her home, either, but I couldn't afford to miss my first day of work.

Later that day, I felt like something was wrong so I called Taylor and told her to go check on Grandma Mae because she wasn't answering her phone. Well, that was the last time I spoke to Grandma Mae and the first time I heard Taylor scream the word "no" like that!

I anxiously waited for Taylor to pick up her phone and talk to me but to no avail. I heard her wailing why over and over again, confirming my worst suspicions. I came to grips with how I was feeling. It was only a matter of time. I hung up the phone, reversed my car out of the garage and headed to the hospital.

CHAPTER 5

Today we laid my brother to rest. The drugs and torment had gotten the best of Aaron. I wish I had told him I loved him one more time before he passed away. My eyes began to well up with tears as I thought about him. It was heartbreaking planning his funeral. Shanice, Taylor and I broke down in tears multiple times throughout the last four days. We consoled each other as much as we could. So many memories we all shared together and separately. We promised each other that we wouldn't bring up any memories of our tumultuous relationship with our father. Unfortunately, most of our greatest memories ended in chaos.

Davis funeral home has provided exceptional funeral services to my family on multiple occasions. They buried my Grandma Mae and my mother.

The day my mother passed away was the day I felt like God had literally taken a part of me. I was empty and extremely hurt. I didn't blame God... I blamed my father. I spoke with my mother daily and visited her every weekend after my father was buried. I even stayed over some nights. On this particular day, I hadn't heard from her. I called her and left a message, telling her that she didn't have to call me back because I'd be over in the morning to take her to breakfast. I woke up early the next morning eager to have breakfast with her. Her birthday was two days away so I thought we'd do a little shopping, too. I called my mother to let her know that I was on my way, but she didn't answer the phone. I figured she was probably outside waiting on me, as she would sometimes do. I pulled up but she wasn't on the front porch. I was hoping she hadn't overslept because it has happened in the past as well. I entered through the back door. Everything was quiet so I called out, "Ma, are you ready?" I still didn't hear anything. Everything seemed normal except for a slight stench coming from her garbage can. I headed towards her bedroom.

The house was immaculate and beautiful. She remodeled after we told her it was too painful to visit her at the house because every piece of furniture brought back the dreadful memories of our childhood. She agreed to remodel once my father passed away so that we would come see her.

I opened her bedroom door and there she was lying in her bed. I walked over towards her. "Ma, get up," I optimistically called out but not too loud to startle her.

My mother didn't move so I stood in front of her and lightly shook her arm as I whispered for her to get up again. Her body was cold and stiff as a board. I was stricken with fear. I withdrew my hand from her arm and quickly put my hands over my mouth attempting to mask my anguished sobs. I fell to my knees and wept in her breast. I wanted just one more day with her.

I never thought I would be back at Davis' Funeral Home ever again once they closed my mother's casket and wheeled her body into the hearse headed to the gravesite.

I forgot how beautiful the funeral home was. The mahogany crown molding and baseboards highlighted the hunter green carpet. There were several antique tables dressed with lace doilies placed right next to different synthetic velvet covered chairs and sofas throughout the rooms. The walls were painted a soft cream that added brightness to an already dark place. It was still elegant. Nothing was out of place.

This place I'm in was very uncomfortable. I felt like my world was closing in on me. So many people showed up for the funeral. I felt like I was suffocating. Aaron was really a good person. I should've been there to help him. He tried to talk to me but I ignored his plea for help. He didn't know that I needed someone to talk to as well. There were times that my past would haunt me for weeks. I would wake up in cold sweats and I even vomited on a couple of occasions. Now, the abuse from my father and Harold haunt me almost daily.

Almost three years to the day Aaron called me. I wasn't going to answer the phone because there was no caller ID and it was around two o'clock in the morning. I didn't answer the first time but he called again. Instead of putting the phone on silent so I could get some rest I decided to answer it. "Hello," I said with the phone barely hanging on my ear.

"Nita?" Aaron whispered.

"Yeah," I responded.

"You sound different," he said. I thought he was on something because he never whispers. "Something is wrong, Juanita," he uttered.

Aaron, what's going on?" I asked and then sighed deeply.

"Dad keeps coming to visit me in my dreams and I'm scared," Aaron cried.

"What do you do any other time," I asked him while yawning. I couldn't help myself because I was

extremely exhausted from working over seventy hours that week.

"I take a pill and then go to sleep," he answered.

Drugs will make you see, say and do some very strange things. "Well, take another pill and call me tomorrow," I suggested. I don't know what happened after that because I woke up and found my phone under my foot. I tried to call him back at the number he called me from but the person who owned the phone told me not to call their phone looking for him. I called back anyway and they hung up on me.

There was a steady flow of people that came out to pay their respects. So many people told me I looked great but what they didn't know was that I was falling apart on the inside. I was so glad the service was finally over.

Dr. Brice texted me today and yesterday, but I didn't respond to any of them. Sometimes I get in this mood where I don't want to talk to anyone. I was mentally and physically tired. I went home and rested up for our family gathering the following day at Uncle Charlie's house. It's a tradition we've held in our family for ages. There was only going to be eight of us there, which was great. We needed to heal and this is how we did it. No outsiders, no friends, just family. We all agreed to meet over Uncle Charlie and Auntie Sophia's house. Their three children Alexandria, Mason and BJ had all flown in to eulogize Aaron. Uncle Charlie is my mother's only sibling. My father alienated them all for years, which made it difficult for us to establish a childhood bond with them. It was heartbreaking not being able to visit my cousins regularly when they only lived a ten-minute drive away.

We ate, napped, watched a couple of movies, laughed and cried. Auntie Sophia prepared so much food. I walked through the living room towards the kitchen to grab another piece of Auntie Sophia's delicious cake when someone knocked on the door. Who could it be? Everyone was already here but I opened the door anyway. There was a petite, young woman at the door with a child that looked about six or seven years old. They both looked familiar but I could not place where I had seen them before.

"Juanita?" she asked. How does she know me?

"Yes, I'm Juanita." I replied.

"We were at Aaron's funeral," she said.

That's where I saw them. How could I forget so quickly? I waited for her to continue because I was a bit embarrassed about not being able to remember her.

"My name is Ann Marie and this is Myles," she said.

Now that I know their names, what are they doing here? Apparently Uncle Charlie or Auntie Sophia knows her.

"I will go get Uncle Charlie," I told her.

I was about to call Uncle Charlie or one of my cousins but I was quickly interrupted.

"Charlie doesn't know about Myles," she responded quickly.

"Uncle Charlie doesn't know about what?" I wondered.

"No one knows," Ann Marie stated.

She looked afraid. I turned to walk away and she tugged at my arm. I turned back to her and could see that this was a serious situation but now is not the time to ruin our family engagement.

"Ann Marie, I'm not sure what your plan is; however, this is not going to happen today. We just buried Aaron and our family needs to heal," I said firmly.

Myles hugged his mother and buried his head in her ribs as she firmly stood her ground. It was clear that she wasn't going to just go away. The conundrum raised by Ann Marie left me perplexed.

"Auntie Sophia will have a heart attack and pass out right on the parlor's floor if she finds out that her husband of thirty-seven years has a child old enough to be her great grandchild," I said to Ann Marie.

Ann Marie laughed. I was puzzled. Oh, she's out for blood now. She was about to say something but I had had enough already. I put my hand on the door and was about to slam it in her face when Uncle Charlie entered the front room.

"Who are you talking to, Juanita?" he asked.

I slowly moved away from the door so he could see them. I was furious with Uncle Charlie. How could he do that to Auntie Sophia?

I overheard my mother on the phone one night while my father was working late. She was crying hysterically. She was trying to be quiet but it woke me up. I opened my bedroom door and listened intently. I wasn't sure who was on the other end of the line but whoever it was, was making my mother very upset. She couldn't stop blowing her nose or conceal her emotions.

"Are you serious?" my mother asked.

"How many months are you?" my mother questioned.

Whatever the lady said caused an outburst of sobbing and profanity. I had never heard my mother swear before.

"Does Lawrence know that you're calling me?" my mother asked angrily. Whatever the caller said

frustrated my mother so badly that she slammed the phone down!

"How could you do this to me, Lawrence?" she uttered to herself in disgust after pounding her fist on the table.

About fifteen minutes later I heard my father come home. I could hear them arguing and shouting in their room. After what occurred that night, I never heard anything else about my father having any illegitimate children.

Ann Marie and Myles did not make one move.

"Hi, Ann Marie and Myles," Uncle Charlie greeted them excitedly with a hug.

Myles leaped into Uncle Charlie's arms. My Uncle was acting as if nothing ever happened. Maybe he didn't know? I need an explanation from both of them at this point. I stood to the side with my arms folded watching the entire interaction. My anger was evident.

"Come on in," Uncle Charlie insisted as he carried Myles into the other room where everyone else was gathered.

I stepped in front of Ann Marie blocking her passage. "What's going on?" I demanded, looking her straight in the eye.

"Everyone needs to know who Myles' father is," she insisted.

"No one needs to know today that Myles is Uncle Charlie's son!" I exclaimed. Just as I was finishing my sentence Auntie Sophia walked into the living room.

"Excuse me!" Auntie Sophia yelled out. She became hysterical and confrontational and walked right up to Ann Marie screaming in her face. "So that's why you would come over regularly all of these years," Auntie Sophia questioned Ann Marie's motives.

"No, no, no! Myles is not Uncle Charlie's baby," she revealed.

"Well, whose son is he then?" I adamantly asked. Uncle Charlie, Miles, Alexandria, Mason, BJ, Shanice and Taylor rushed over to see what was going on.

"Aaron's," Ann Marie replied. "Miles is Aaron's son."

I felt like a complete fool. I should not have assumed anything. I could see the relief on Auntie Sophia's face.

"Ms. Sophia, I would never do such a thing," Ann Marie voiced in humility

"I'm so sorry. I just heard what Juanita said and immediately I was stunned and felt manipulated," Auntie Sophia confessed with her hands on her heart.

Everyone wanted to know what was going on and since I made the accusations, I thought it would be prudent if I explained what had just transpired.

Ann Marie and Myles stayed with us for the rest of the day and we all shared stories of Aaron. The revelation of Aaron's offspring made the family gathering even more special. We laughed, cried, ate, embraced and shared story after story until it was time to leave. Shanice and Taylor communicated that they would see me tomorrow as we planned to go away together for a few days.

I gladly drove Ann Marie and Myles home. She shared copious details of her time with Aaron. I promised her that I would touch base with them later and waited for them to enter their apartment before driving off.

> The architectural makeup of Ann Marie's apartment building reminded me of Dynasty apartments where Grandma Mae moved after the fire. She was really nervous when she first moved into Dynasty Apartments. This was her first move since Grandpa Teddy passed away and second time moving after leaving home from college. She took me with her to pick up her keys. The two-bedroom apartment was beautiful and exciting for me because Grandma Mae said the extra room was for all of her grandkids

except for me. In sadness, I tugged on her sleeve and asked her where I was going to sleep. She brought me to her bedroom door and pointed. "Here," she stated.

"But this is your bedroom, Grandma Mae," I responded in confusion.

"Our room," she confirmed. She put her finger over her lips. I repeated her gesture and smiled. Her secret was safe with me.

I drove off and headed home. I stopped at the first intersection and smiled. Having a nephew felt surreal and extraordinary. I heard a horn beeping and then someone called my name. I turned around to my left and Gabriel was waving to me. Oh my goodness, I look like a mess. My tears had erased all traces of my makeup. I have lipstick and foundation on both of my shoulders and suit collar from embracing my family. I just looked plain ole disheveled and there was nothing I could do about it. Gabriel signaled me to pull over in a parking lot just ahead. We both got out of our cars. Gabriel approached me with open arms like we had been friends forever. I stretched out my hand; he caught my cue and shook my hand instead. I apologized for my disheveled appearance and explained that I was grieving the death of my only brother. He extended his condolences and asked if there was anything he could do. I said, "No." We chatted briefly. I inadvertently mentioned that I was hungry so he invited me to grab an early dinner. I accepted his dinner invitation. Although I was famished and drained, I still needed to eat.

I ran a few errands and then I stopped at the mall to purchase a new outfit for dinner tonight.

I was finally home and I couldn't wait to get in the shower. I thought about Gabriel and what we might talk about tonight when Dr. Brice ran across my mind. I grinned. No one should ever know what I'm thinking about exactly when I think about Dr. Brice... not even Dr. Brice. I turned on some music to ease the mood. I frittered away some time looking for the perfect accessories for my new outfit. Here I am on a sabbatical and I'm more stressed out than when I was working eleven-hour days. I was mentally and physically tired but I had already told Gabriel yes.

I decided not to wear heels so I wouldn't entice Gabriel. Like I said, "He's not really my type"! This was great because I wanted the company without a commitment. The phone rang as I was headed to the door. "Hello," I answered.

"Hi, Juanita, this is Kingston," he said.

"Kingston and not Dr. Brice? Is something wrong?" I replied.

"How come you haven't texted me back?" he questioned me. I told him that I had to go and that I didn't owe him an explanation. I hope I didn't offend him. At this point, I was very hungry and anxious to meet up with Gabriel instead of eating alone.

I was about to hang up when Dr. Brice said, "May I ask where are you going?"

I didn't want him to ask too many questions. I just wanted to go to dinner to eat and have a good time. "I'm going to dinner," I asserted.

"Can I ask..." he began to ask.

Before he could finish asking his question I interjected. "Kingston, no you cannot ask." I declared.

"I'm sorry, I'll see you tomorrow," he stated.

I paused for a second and then found myself apologizing for sounding so harsh. I just didn't want him to know I was going out to dinner with another man. I hung up the phone. I will see him tomorrow and apologize again before leaving with my sisters.

I quickly looked in the mirror and then I looked again. I took a minute admiring how I looked and I must say I looked "HOT"! As I turned away from the mirror, I realized I actually looked at myself in the mirror and didn't see my mother nor did a triggered memory trap me into running away from the mirror and into a traumatic instance.

I arrived at the restaurant and strutted in. Gabriel spotted me walking in and got up to escort me the rest of the way to the table. He pulled out my chair and tried to push it in but it got stuck. "I got it," I chuckled.

Gabriel was quite charming. I found myself giggling like a schoolgirl. He told me as a kid he had nightmares about his aunt that used to eat bugs. He said he would have these recurring dreams that she went to kiss him and his head turned into a horse fly. I almost wet my panties. Of course, I couldn't tell him that. He complimented me on my dress. I'm glad he did because I love the attention. He looked at me the way Dr. Brice does. I wish it were Dr. Brice sitting at this table across from me... sigh.

The night was finally over and I could not stop smiling. He walked me to my car and kissed my hand before we parted ways. I didn't know guys still did that. Dr. Brice practiced chivalry; however, Gabriel just took it up a notch.

I went to grab my phone to call Dr. Brice and realized I left it on the table. I ran back into the restaurant. Thank God it was still there. On my way back to my car I saw Dr. Brice with that older woman again. They must've gone to a neighboring restaurant. I hope he didn't see Gabriel and me together.

"Who is she?" I whispered to myself. I hid between two cars so he couldn't see me. I watched him walk her to her car, he kissed her on her cheek and she got in. It must not be that serious because it was only a kiss on the cheek. Dr. Brice looked very handsome. He then got into his car that was parked right next to the woman's car. I watched him drive off before I moved out from hiding between the cars. I hurried into my car and pulled off, smiling. I couldn't believe that I went out with one of the most charismatic men I've ever met in a long time. However, the man I really want, I keep rejecting.

I was almost home when my gaslight came on. I pulled into the nearest gas station and I was about to get out when I got a text notification. I grabbed my phone. To my surprise, Gabriel was checking to see if I made it home safely. "That's nice of you," I texted him back. He then texted me back asking If I would call him when I got home. Why does he want more than I'm willing to give him? He thinks he can apply slow pressure to lure me in. It's not going to work. I told him I'd text him when I got home.

Before I could send my text to Gabriel, I was frightened by a knock on my window. It was Dr. Brice.

"Would you like for me to pump your gas?" he asked me.

"Please," I replied. I decided to get out and keep him company while he pumped my gas. He couldn't stop looking at my dress. I couldn't stop looking at him.

"Is this what you wore to dinner?" he inquired.

I was sizing him up before I answered his question.

"Yes," I replied.

I knew he wanted to ask who I went to dinner with but I wasn't going to volunteer that information either. I leaned on the car while he pumped my gas. He asked me if I enjoyed my dinner and I said yes. "So, what are you doing out this late?" I asked as I began to twirl my hair.

"I went out to dinner, too," he stated.

I smiled. I know he was waiting for me to ask him who he went to dinner with but I already know. Dr. Brice finished pumping my gas. He insisted on paying for it even though I pleaded with him not to. I was about to get in my car when he said, "You want to catch a movie?"

"But it's late," I answered. Plus, I'm still grieving my brother's death," I mumbled so he couldn't hear me.

"Come on, Ms. Winfield," he begged.

The way he said "Ms. Winfield" made my stomach flutter. I just finished having dinner with another man and was now going to the movies with Dr. Brice. This is turning into a love triangle. "Okay," I said without hesitation.

It didn't even matter what we were going to see. I was completely mesmerized. If he called out Ms. Winfield one more time "ain't" no telling what was going to happen. We might not even make it to the movies. You know, my back seats fold down.

One minute my life went from abusive and tumultuous relationships, to dinner and the movies with two different men in the same night. I really welcomed all of this attention because it kept my mind off Aaron and other issues.

Dr. Brice suggested I drive home and park my car because he didn't want me driving home by myself after the movies. I grabbed my purse and shawl; and handed it to Dr. Brice and told him I needed to go in the house for a minute. I ran in the house and put on the heels that I hadn't worn to dinner with Gabriel. I'm wearing them for who I bought them for, Dr. Brice. I strutted out of my home hoping that he would immediately take notice of my shoes. I made eye contact with him when I walked out of the door and his eyes were instantly drawn to my shoes. He smiled and then tucked his lips in. I saw his ears move. That was different and I like it. Every ounce of flirtation matters to me.

He opened the passenger door to his car and waited for me to get in. As I got into his car, he complimented me on my shoes. Dr. Brice always gives me compliments. That is one thing I really like about him. A woman needs to know she looks good. Kingston doesn't have a problem letting me know that.

We drove to the cinema that was a few blocks away from my home. He parked in the parking lot right next to the building. He was about to get out and I said, "Wait a minute." Dr. Brice closed his door and stared into my eyes.

"Yes, Ms. Winfield," he answered.

I melted. I should not say anything so he could repeat my name again. "I don't want to see a movie," I announced.

"Okay, if not a movie, then what would you like to do?" he inquired.

"Perhaps we can go to the lake?" I suggested. I really like the lake and didn't have the opportunity to go there this week. Besides, I don't think I had enough energy to stay awake throughout the entire movie. He seemed a bit hesitant but I think he just wanted to be in my company so he politely agreed.

On our way to the lake we stopped at a local pizzeria so I could use the restroom. Dr. Brice got out of the car and watched me go in. Wow, this was a new standard of treatment that I could and want to get used to. I rushed to the ladies' room because I couldn't hold it in. I had just used the bathroom at home too. There was someone exiting the restroom as I entered. The lady looked very familiar. As I was passing her, she asked me if I was Aaron's sister and I told her I was. The lady extended her condolences and then mentioned how beautiful the funeral ceremony was. She then said she dated Aaron briefly but I couldn't remember who she was for the life of me. "I'm Angelina Brewer," she said. She must've noticed I

Aaron brought Angelina and his best friend, Robert, over to the house after school one day. I told Aaron that Robert wasn't a true friend and I heard Robert flirts with Angelina when he's not around.

"So, she's mine," Aaron said.

I told Aaron to be careful. Well, on this particular day at the house Aaron left them in his room while he went to the bathroom. Robert decided that this was his opportunity to put the moves on her at our house like some fool. I was in the bathroom so Aaron went back to the room and on his way he heard Angelina tell Robert to stop before she tells Aaron.

Aaron walked to his bedroom door and curiously said, "Tell Aaron what?"

Aaron startled them and he saw Angelina push Robert off of her. Aaron picked up his nun chucks and started swinging them at Robert. Angelina kept screaming for Aaron to stop but Aaron wouldn't. I ran in the room and pulled him off of Robert. Aaron knocked out Robert's front tooth and broke his nose. That was the last I saw of Robert and Angelina and the first time I saw my father's rage manifest through my brother.

I thanked Angelina for her kind words. She hugged me, which I think she needed more than I did, and wished me all the best. She walked away and I went to use the restroom. As I was on my way back to the car, I noticed Dr. Brice talking to someone. I almost headed out the door before I recognized who it was. How does Dr. Brice know Gabriel? I stepped away from the door but not far enough where I couldn't see what was going on. Dr. Brice and Gabriel were standing in front of Dr. Brice's car talking and laughing.

A few minutes later they shook hands and Gabriel drove off. Dr. Brice headed in so I went to the bathroom door and turned around as if I had just finished up.

"Is everything okay?" Dr. Brice asked.

"Yes, there was a line to use the restroom" I replied with a smile. He grabbed my hand and kissed me on the cheek. "How many times do we have to go through this?" I thought to myself. He is really persistent.

"Would you like a drink?" he asked before we made it out the door.

"Sure, I'll have tonic water with lemon," I said cheerfully. We grabbed a window seat. I had forgotten how beautiful things were in the nightlight. He sat right next to me rather than across from me, which I thought was rather cute. He put his arm on the back of my chair and bent over to say something to me.

"I have feelings for you and I can't stop thinking about you," he whispered in my ear. I was flattered. The feelings were mutual but somewhat confusing and complicated. I know I seem desperate but I'm lonely and depressed. What I don't want to do is sleep with just anyone just for the sake of company or to feel as if I'm wanted. Sex with this one, sex with that one isn't lady like. I'm human and I have needs, too, but I really wanted to make sure this time the love was real and safe. The only way I can go all the way with Dr. Brice is if there's potential for marriage. I want to give this special someone every part of me and I want that back.

Dr. Brice excused himself to go to the men's room. I watched him walk. He had on a gray suit, with a blue V-neck sweater and a pair of Sebago Salem Oxfords. He disappeared into the restroom as a text alert rang on my phone. I glanced down to a message from Gabriel checking to see if I had made it home safely. I deleted the message that I didn't finish earlier and I replied, "I'm safe." I waited to see what he had to say, but there wasn't a reply to my text because he decided to call me. I looked to see if Dr. Brice was coming out of the restroom and then I looked at the phone again. Instead of answering Gabriel's call, I texted him back saying, "It's late, Gabriel, call me tomorrow." He apologized and said okay. I turned my phone to vibrate and put it in my purse. "It's nice to be pursued," I thought. However, I didn't like the fact that they both seemed to know each other very well.

Dr. Brice made his way back to the table. Only this time he sat across from me and stared into my eyes. I could tell he wanted to say something serious. Actually, I wanted to bite his bottom lip. I wasn't ready to reject him again. I just wanted to hang out with him without having to commit to him either. If I'm really honest, I'm afraid this won't work.

"What do you want?" Dr. Brice inquired. I was shocked because I wasn't expecting him to be bold like this. I wondered if he knew I went out with someone else tonight.

"What do you mean what do I want?" I replied. He reached out for my hands but I didn't respond. I put my head down. This does seem like a high school game but it was not. I wanted him but now is not the right time. I know I sound like a tape recorder but it's the truth. Who is he? Who am I? I can tell he was frustrated at this time.

"Come on, let's go," he insisted.

He got up, took my hand and he rushed me out. I thought we were headed to the lake but instead he took me back home. He pulled up to my door and put the car in park. I could see him turning his head my way. I looked over at him after I grabbed my purse as I put my hand on the door handle. "I'm sorry if I upset you," I said sadly. He had this confused look on his face.

"I'm not upset," Dr. Brice said.

"I thought we were going to the lake?" I questioned him.

"We are going to the lake. You'll need your swimsuit, right?" Dr. Brice stated.

"I can't swim," I said after I laughed out loud.

"Then why did you want to go to the lake?" he asked curiously.

"I figured we would talk and walk along the sand," I answered and then shrugged my shoulders.

"I can teach you how to swim." Dr. Brice said earnestly.

"REALLY!" I exclaimed.

"Yes, really," Dr. Brice assured me.

I was speechless. How did he know I wanted to learn how to swim? I can't wait.

I went into the house and slipped on my favorite swimsuit with a wrap and rushed back out. Dr. Brice was listening to some Marvin Gaye when I returned to the car. I smiled. "I love Marvin Gaye!" I exclaimed when I closed the car door.

"Me too," he said with a grand smile on his face. We sang 'What's Going On" together. Dr. Brice can sing pretty well, too. I was definitely impressed after hearing him sing for the second time.

We were almost to the lake and I was becoming extremely nervous. "Where are his swimming trunks?" I thought to myself.

"I have a pair of gym shorts in the trunk if you're wondering what I'm going to wear," he stated as if he knew what I was thinking.

"I was just thinking that," I divulged.

We arrived at the lake and parked. It was dark but the moonlight gave off this ambiance that was perfect for someone to feel a sense of romance.

"Wait right here," Dr. Brice said before he got out of the car and went into his trunk to grab his shorts.

He left the trunk open so he could change with some privacy. When he had finished, he closed the trunk and came back around to open my door. He held out his hand and I instantly melted inside as I placed my hand in his.

"Are you ready?" he asked with a curious look on his face.

"I guess," I answered as I got out of the car and he took off my swimsuit wrap. I told him, I don't think it's wise to try and teach someone how to swim at night. He agreed but he still wanted us to go in the water.

"We don't have to go too far out," he suggested.

I started walking toward the water and intentionally walked ahead of him a little. I know he was watching my butt shake. I wanted to get wet first so I walked until the water was at my waist. The water was a little chilly but warm enough to get in. I wanted to just immerse myself in the water but I didn't. He walked up behind me and wrapped his arms around my waist.

"Are you okay?" he whispered?

I didn't move nor answer him because I wanted him next to me. I could feel his excitement. He couldn't hide his arousal. My heart started beating faster. It's not like I've never done this before. Just knowing what could possibly happen intensified the moment. I felt his hands moving from my waist up to my breast. I didn't stop him. He softly and slowly kissed my neck repeatedly. We both couldn't resist this moment. I turned around to face him and he pulled me close to him and we began to fervently kiss.

I felt that things were going too fast and too soon so I pulled away. I took a deep breath and just looked at him waiting for him to say something. He looked at me trying to figure out what he was doing wrong. "I'm not ready for this, Kingston," I put my hands together in a praying position over my lips. "I don't know much, if anything, about you," I softly spoke after removing my hands from my mouth. I put my head down.

"I don't have parents," he said after a few seconds.

I went to live with my aunt after my parents died in a boating accident," he continued.

After a long pause he said, "I don't talk much because I'm so used to listening and observing."

He's finally opening up to me. Should I just let him talk and only interject when it was necessary? That's what I did.

"I don't sleep around with women for ego sake. A lot of women come to see me to talk about their abuse and how it has affected them. Most of the time sex and unfaithfulness is a key factor or the major subject leading to the abuse. I don't want that. What I do want is you," he said.

Dr. Brice just said a mouthful. Then he gently held me. My face rested on his muscular chest. His heart was beating so fast. He gently placed his face on my head.

"I want you, Juanita," he repeated.

What do I say? I didn't know how to respond. I wasn't getting any swimming lessons tonight but I sure was wet. It was okay. I wanted to be here with him just as much as he wanted to be here with me.

He put his hands on my face and slowly placed his lips on mine. He turned us around and he backed up closer to the shore. He lay down on the sand and tenderly pulled me on top of him. We lay in less than a half-foot of water and made out like teenagers. He began to caress my body and we were about to go all the way until what looked like a group of college students started yelling and screaming. About two hundred feet away, they were splashing in the water and acting wild.

"I guess it wasn't meant to be," he sighed.

"It will happen if and when the time is right," I said. We sat up and talked for a while on the lake's shore and then we left. I was glad nothing happened. Marriage is my goal.

CHAPTER 6

My therapy appointment is in three hours and I can't wait to see Dr. Brice. I'm up and dressed. I can't get my mind off of what almost happened last night. I'm going to tell him today that I need him and this will be my last appointment. I haven't been thinking about my past lately because, well, I don't know why.

I'm not even sure what we're going to talk about today. That's if we talk at all. I needed to pick up a few things for my weekend get-a-way with my sisters before my therapy appointment. I picked up my purse and was about to walk out the door when I got a text notification from Gabriel asking if he could take me out later today. I would ask where he is taking me but it doesn't matter because I won't be there. I'll be enjoying some quality time with my sisters! I do recall telling him that I will be leaving for the weekend. Before I could answer his text my phone rings. It's Gabriel. Why does he even bother texting if he's going to turn around and call?

"Hey Gabriel," I answered with slight enthusiasm.

"Hi, Juanita," Gabriel says, sounding like a super sexy Tom Jones. "Stay focused," I said to myself. I could hear him breathing.

"I can't stop thinking about you," he said.

Oh, my goodness, he sounds like Dr. Brice. I didn't know what to say. Now he has me thinking about Dr. Brice.

"Are you still there?" he asked.

"Yes, I'm here Gabriel," I confirmed.

"Did you hear me? I said I can't stop thinking about you," he repeated.

He sounded a bit annoyed that he had to repeat himself. Where is he going with all of this flattery?

"I heard you. I didn't know how to answer you," I said bluntly.

"I know I'm a little forward but I couldn't help but tell you what you're doing to me," Gabriel said before clearing his throat.

What am I doing to him? I haven't done anything yet nor do I plan to make him feel the way he does about me. He probably has sex with women an hour after meeting them. Because I'm not falling all over him, is probably driving him mad. I know men love a good chase.

"Can I take you shopping later today?" he asked.

Thank goodness I was leaving with my sisters because if I weren't, I would be in Dr. Brice's arms, not Gabriel's.

I didn't want to disappoint Gabriel by telling him no but that's what I have to do. Wait...I'm not disappointing him on purpose. I really have somewhere to go.

"Gabriel, I'll be away this weekend." I reminded him. He sighed. I thought I was in the clear.

"Oh... okay, well how about when you return?" he asked.

I knew he was disappointed when I told him I couldn't. He hadn't planned for that nor did I plan for him to extend the invitation to the next week.

"We will talk about it when I get back," I insisted.

"I guess I'll have to find out when you get back then," he said saddened.

I know I wasn't being very cooperative but I'm not about to apologize for it either. The attraction is superficial. I'm not even trying to seduce, lure or entice him and I can't get him away from me. Is this the trick to getting what I want from men?

"I'm headed to the mall right now so I can prepare for my trip," I said as I tried to rush him off the phone. He started to say something but I cut him off and told him I would call him when I get back in town. I hung up before he could utter another word.

After I got off the phone with Gabriel I headed straight to the mall and picked up everything I needed. Before I left the mall, I stopped at the fragrance and cosmetic department in Macys to pick up some perfume. I wanted to smell enticing. I wanted something new. Something that would make Dr. Brice aroused during my entire appointment with him. The sales clerk recommended some perfume with a name that would make a whale blush. Heck, I wanted to love myself after smelling it on my arm. I bought it and layered it on like lotion once I got to the car.

I arrived early for my appointment. I had time to kill so I stopped at the café across the street from Dr. Brice's office. I purchased a latte and sat quietly at a corner table next to a window. I sipped my latte as I waited for the time to pass. I haven't "people watched" in a long time. Life has been so hectic over the years that I forgot how to really stop and enjoy everything around me. I was comfortable and the view was perfect. Suddenly I could feel someone standing over me but I didn't turn around to see who it was. Okay, now I had to turn around and see because the shadow was still there. I knew someone was watching me. I looked up and this thin man, with a dark, thick beard and shoulder length hair flowing like Fabio smiled at me. His eyelashes were perfect. I pay almost a hundred dollars every two weeks to get mine to look like his... incredible.

"Excuse me," he said once our eyes connected.

"Yes?" I responded questioningly.

"Is anyone sitting here?" he asked.

I glanced over at the empty seat in front of me and then around the cafe to see if there were any other vacant seats. There were plenty of places he could sit. Apparently, I didn't know I had the best seat in the house. All I wanted to do was see Dr. Brice. I looked back up to the man and he smiled again. I ran my hand through my hair and pulled it over to one side.

"Can I sit with you?" he asked.

"Sure," I replied with a smile.

"Are you waiting on someone?" he asked.

Okay, so he's trying to pick me up. Although this man sitting across from me was very attractive, I didn't want to be bothered. I was completely smitten by Dr. Brice. After about two minutes into our conversation, he mentioned how good I smelled. Look, if my new perfume is picking up complete strangers, I know Dr. Brice is about to ask me to marry him after one whiff.

I waited for the time to elapse like a kid waiting for summer vacation. My conversation with the man was very casual and he could see I wasn't interested in anything beyond a cup of coffee.

I decided to head up to Dr. Brice's office. I wished the man a great day and quickly walked across the street. I was so anxious to see Dr. Brice. Diane told me to just go ahead up to his office. We've established a mutual friendship so there was no need for her to check if I could go up. Well, that's what I assumed. When I arrived at the fourteenth floor the waiting room was empty. Maureen welcomed me with a smile. She was on the phone and motioned for me to have a seat.

I could hear her trying to keep the conversation with the patient on the phone confidential the best she could. "Abigail, just settle down. Dr. Brice will see you tomorrow," Maureen calmly said. I glanced over at Maureen. I could tell she was trying her best to keep the situation under control. "No, you cannot come in today," Maureen firmly stated. "If it's an emergency then call 911," Maureen replied.

I don't know how Maureen does it. I'm sure some of Dr. Brice's patients are battling schizophrenia and many other psychological issues.

"You've called here three times, Abigail, and I can't help you," Maureen said confidently.

I drifted off from Maureen's conversation when I had an overwhelming sensation to go to the bathroom. That darn waterfall always awakens my bladder. I headed straight for the restroom. As I was about to flush the toilet, I heard voices coming from Dr. Brice's office. I can't believe I'm about to eavesdrop again. I pressed my ear to the wall. "I don't know what is happening to me!" the voice exclaimed. Okay, it was clearly a man talking with Dr. Brice and something about his voice was vaguely familiar.

"It must be serious," Dr. Brice said.

"She's beautiful, she's smart, and she appears to be interested in me," the man responded with uncertainty.

"No way, this can't be who I think it is," I whispered.

"Have you told her how you feel about her?" Dr. Brice asked?

"No, not specifically. She might think I'm crazy because I haven't known her that long," the man replied.

"Gabriel, I think you should tell her how you feel anyway so you'll know where she stands," Dr. Brice advised.

I quickly put my hand over my mouth so they wouldn't hear me gasp! I was super paranoid. I looked around to make sure there were no cameras in the bathroom. Then I remembered that cameras in public restrooms are against the law.

I am trapped in this bathroom. There's no place else to go. I can't let Gabriel see me here nor can Dr. Brice know that I know Gabriel. I hope Maureen doesn't come knocking on the door to check up on me.

My thought process was interrupted when I heard the man in Dr. Brice's office crying. "Oh Lord. Gabriel cannot be crying," I muttered to myself. How old is he? He's just way too sensitive for me.

Gabriel then asks, "What if she doesn't want me?"

"Then you move on," Dr. Brice stated. I then heard Dr. Brice end his session and let Gabriel know that he'll get through this.

I'm so glad I kept my eyes on Dr. Brice. Although I can't put my finger on it, after listening to Gabriel in there I realize there's something not quite right with him. I waited to hear Dr. Brice's door open so I could time how long it would take Gabriel to get on the elevator. All of sudden, someone knocked on the bathroom door. My eyes grew and my heart began to pound. It startled me. Oh, my goodness, is that Gabriel at the door? I didn't know if I should talk. "I'm so busted," I thought. Then there was another knock. I was about to disguise my voice when I heard a woman say, "Are you alright?"

"Yes, I'll be right out," I whispered loud enough for the woman on the other side to hear me. If it wasn't Maureen on the other side of the door then who could it be? I didn't hear anything coming from Dr. Brice's office. Had the two men walked out together? I waited as long as I could before I eased out of the bathroom. To my surprise no one was waiting at the door. I slowly walked back to the waiting room to find it empty. Maureen was gone. Dr. Brice's door was closed. Do I knock on his door or do I wait?

After pacing the floor in the waiting room for about five minutes, I walked over to Dr. Brice's door and knocked nervously. My hands were trembling. I didn't hear him say wait a minute nor did I hear him walking to the door. I took a deep breath. Is he okay? Where did everyone disappear to? Why is he not answering his door? Do I knock again? I could either leave or knock one more time and if Dr. Brice doesn't open his door I can try and see if it's open. Then it hit me, why don't I just call him? I made up my mind to just leave. I felt awkward standing here and waiting for him to open the door when I was pretty sure he was in there. I turned around and headed toward the elevators when all of a sudden, the office door swung open. I turned around to see Dr. Brice on his phone looking at me holding up his index finger signaling me to wait. I stood at the elevators, rolled my eyes and pressed the down button.

"Please hold on!" Dr. Brice said to the person on the phone. He put the phone down and walked to the elevator where I was just about to step in it.

"Where are you going?" he asked.

How dare he ask me where I am going? He has an awesome secretary so I know he knows that I have an appointment today.

"I've been waiting on you," I said and folded my arms belligerently.

"But your appointment isn't for another twenty-five minutes?" he stated in confusion. I reached for my phone to check my appointment and I noticed that I was indeed a half hour early. I was mortified.

"How could I have gotten my appointment wrong?" I thought to myself. I sighed deeply. Dr. Brice waited for my response.

"Oh, no, I don't know how I botched up the time of my appointment," I said apologetically.

"It's okay," he said optimistically.

"Maureen didn't say anything to you before she left?" he questioned.

I didn't know Maureen was leaving. I was in the bathroom and I'm not about to tell him that. I am already embarrassed.

"No, I wasn't in the waiting area when she left," I said.

"I apologize," he replied.

Dr. Brice asked me if I could wait for him to finish up with his phone client and I agreed. I slowly moved away from the elevators and went back to sit down in the waiting area as I watched Dr. Brice walk back into his office. I sat there in shame trying to figure out how I confused the time. While I was waiting for him, I heard him yell out, "I won't forgive you!" I'm sure he deals with all types of personalities, but I think it was that older woman he normally sees just before me.

After about fifteen minutes, he opened the office door and signaled for me to enter. He closed the door behind us and escorted me to the sofa. I wanted to just jump all over him, but it appeared that he was distracted by something. His entire disposition was off. It was nothing like I'm accustomed to. I think it had something to do with the person he'd been talking to on the phone.

Dr. Brice wouldn't look at me. His back was towards me and he rustled through some papers on his desk. Some of the papers cascaded to the floor like feathers. Immediately frustrated, he slammed his hand on his desk. I jumped and gasped. Then he stopped. I know he heard me.

"I apologize," he whispered with his back still towards me.

I didn't say a word.

I recall my father punching a hole right through our living room wall after my mother told him she was pregnant with Aaron. He was livid. She didn't get pregnant on her own so I don't know why he got so angry.

After he pulled his hand out of the wall, he was even angrier. My mother turned white as a ghost. I could see the fear in her eyes. I didn't move. Taylor and Shanice were over Grandma Mae's house, which was a good thing because they would have been crying and that would have set him off even more.

"You did this on purpose! I told you I didn't want any more kids," he yelled.

I will never forget his words. My mother just kept shaking her head no and saying no. "I'm so sorry, Lawrence," she cried.

"Get rid of it!" he demanded. He walked past her and intentionally rammed his shoulder into hers knocking her against the wall.

"I'll be right back," Dr. Brice said and excused himself.

He walked inside his personal bathroom and shut the door. I quickly ran over to the door and I could hear him sobbing. I knocked on the door and asked him if everything was okay.

"I'll be right out," he said as he tried to disguise his emotions.

I knew he wasn't okay so I slowly opened the door and he was sitting on the toilet with his face in his hands. He slowly removed his hands from his eyes. He looked up at me with the most pitiful look I've ever seen on a man. I was broken. I knew something was very wrong and there was nothing I could do about it.

"I'm sorry, Juanita," he said. His voice was shaky while his tears were dropping to the floor.

I closed the bathroom door behind me, walked up to him and held him. He tucked his head into my stomach and wrapped his hand around my right thigh just under my butt. He began crying even harder. Dr. Brice needed me more than I needed him.

After holding him for several minutes I knelt down and looked into his eyes.

"I'm here for you, Kingston," I whispered. "I don't know what's going on but I do know pain when I see it," I said as I ran my hand through his hair.

Seeing him cry made me want to cry but I didn't want to take the focus off his situation. I know he's not supposed to show this side of himself to me but we have more than just a doctor patient relationship. I wiped the tears away from his cheeks and then kissed him. He tried to get into it but he couldn't. He stopped kissing me and then held me tighter.

"Juanita," he whispered in my ear.

I waited for him to say something else but he didn't. Instead he started to cry even more. I felt bad for kissing him because it was as if I were taking advantage of his situation. I just squeezed him back. After holding him for about two to three minutes I got up and kissed his forehead.

"I have to go, Kingston," I said.

"I know," he replied.

I grabbed my purse and I left. I entered the elevator and the door closed. I cried once I was safely out of his sight. Who is hurting him? To see a grown man cry was awful. It's like seeing someone hurt my baby brother, Aaron.

Joey, one of the kids from next door, loved getting Aaron all riled up. He would play mean and nasty tricks on Aaron. Aaron would get so angry he would begin to stutter profusely, which frustrated him even more. Once Joey found out that when Aaron was furious it caused him to stutter, Joey made it his goal to antagonize Aaron for pleasure. Joey would laugh at Aaron stuttering as Aaron would chase and yell at Joey. Aaron would come in the house crying and Mom would try to calm him down so she could understand what he was trying to say. I couldn't help him. I couldn't protect him and it hurt me to the core.

Once Mom knew what was going on, she approached Joey's parents but they were in denial about what their son was doing.

One of our neighbors discovered that Aaron had a stuttering problem and helped him overcome that handicap, which he also had suffered from himself.

Eventually, Joey and his family moved from the neighborhood but that couldn't undo all the pain Joey had already inflicted on Aaron.

I made it out to my car and just sat in it for a few minutes. I felt horrible for leaving Dr. Brice like that because I knew he would stay with me had I been in that situation.

I decided to call my sisters and I told them I would meet them at the hotel in the morning. Taylor and Shanice were vehemently against going ahead of me and they insisted on waiting for me so we all could drive up together. No questions asked... I really love my sisters.

I got out of the car and went back to Dr. Brice's office. I couldn't stop feeling terrible for leaving him up there alone. I was anxious to get back to him. As I got on the elevator my phone rang. It was Gabriel.

"What does Gabriel want now?" I said to myself.

I tried to silence the call but accidently hit the green phone icon answering it instead. How could I make such a stupid mistake? I was instantly annoyed.

"Hello, hello? Juanita?" I heard him calling my name before I could even put the phone to my ear.

"What's up Gabriel," I questioned him.

"I meant to ask you when are you getting back?" he asked.

Oh, my goodness he sounds extremely desperate.

"I'll be back home late Sunday night." I said.

"Okay, I'll call you on Monday to set something up," he stated.

"All right, I will talk to you then," I said before I hung up.

"He wants this badly," I said and laughed out loud before realizing that I had not disconnected the call. I quickly tapped the "end call" icon, effectively terminating the call. Oh well, I hope he hadn't heard me.

I went up to Dr. Brice's office and noticed his office door was still ajar. I walked towards his bathroom and saw him still sitting on the toilet. He was still crying because I heard him sniffling. He has to tell me what's going on. I'm not sure if he's trying to deceive me or if he needs a therapist himself.

"Dr. Brice," I called out before entering the bathroom.

"Yes," he replied and still emotional. I slowly walked in the bathroom and he was still sitting on the toilet wiping his nose. I wet a paper towel and blotted his face. He wasn't even ashamed. He grabbed my hand, pulled me onto his lap, wrapped his arms around my waist and placed his head on my breast. I embraced him back and waited.

"You can't stay in here all day," I said firmly.

I removed his arms from around my waist and stood up, extending my hand out for him to take it. He hesitated like a stubborn child. I refused to let him stay in the funk he was in so I left my hand out until he accepted my invitation. He took my hand and I led him out of the bathroom. I grabbed his keys, locked up his office and we got on the elevator together. We didn't say a word to each other. As we stood side-by-side, I reached for his hand and he met me halfway with his own. "Why are we playing these high school games?" I thought to myself.

Without notice he pulled me over to him and looked me in the eyes and said, "When you come back from your trip with your sisters we need to talk."

I hope he's going to talk about what's going on with him because I already know he desires to be with me. I also need to know what he is looking for in a relationship because I'm not sixteen so if it's just sex, we both should move on.

The elevator reached the lobby and the door slid open smoothly. The woman I saw Dr. Brice with was waiting there and she stepped into the elevator, blocking our exit. Dr. Brice immediately tensed up and let go of my hand. Maybe now I will find out who this lady is.

"Gwen, this is not the time," Dr. Brice said to the woman.

So now I know her name.

Gwen turned and looked at me and exclaimed, "So you're the one!"

What is she talking about? What has Dr. Brice been saying to her about me?

"You've turned him against me, haven't you?" she yelled.

I was two seconds away from saying something to her that I have not said to someone older than me in a long time. Before I could open my mouth Dr. Brice quickly stepped between the two of us. It was as if he knew she was capable of being violent. Suddenly she pushed him out of the way and grabbed me by my hair and slapped me. I was in complete shock. She really caught me by surprise. I tried to move out of the way, but apparently my reaction was a bit slow because Dr. Brice pulled her off of me before I could even move. Dr. Brice pinned her against the opposite side of the elevator. Gwen was out of control and acting like a maniac.

The elevator door opened again and a woman was about to enter but noticed that something wasn't right so she backed up and the doors closed again.

"What is wrong with you?" Dr. Brice angrily asked Gwen.

"I didn't do anything to you!" I screamed in her face.

I kicked off my heels and swung at Gwen almost jabbing her in the face. I felt the need to defend myself because she kept swinging at me even though Dr. Brice was trying his best to block her. The elevator door opened again and Dr. Brice forced Gwen off on the sixth floor. The elevator then descended to the lobby. My face was red and irritated where she had slapped me. I still couldn't believe what had just happened. It was unbelievable.

"You need to control your patient?" I said furiously.

"I'm sorry," he sadly said.

"I knew all this was a mistake," I asserted.

He was about to say something before the elevator door opened to the lobby. I looked around to see if I saw Gwen but there was no sign of her. I was furious and embarrassed.

"I didn't know this was going to happen," he said tenderly.

"Who is she is what I want to know?" I declared as I walked heatedly to my car. I was going to stop and force him to tell me everything I needed to know. However, I knew I wasn't ready to hear anything right now because I was fuming. I finally reached my car and I got in. I turned to say something to Dr. Brice and out of the corner of my eye I saw Gwen approaching us again.

"Get rid of her!" I commanded.

"I can't just do that. You won't understand," Dr. Brice replied.

"No, I don't!" I exclaimed and drove off. I pulled over about half a mile away to cry. I didn't ask for any of this. I decided to just go ahead and tell my sisters to pick me up tonight so we could head out of town. Before I could call them, Dr. Brice called my phone.

"Doesn't he know that I don't want to talk to him?" I said aloud to myself and I answered the phone anyway.

"What do you want?" I yelled into the phone.

"Please don't yell at me, Juanita," he asked.

If he were right here right now, I would strangle him.

"Are you crying?" he questioned.

"Kingston, why do you need to know?" I asked in anger.

I was on the car phone so I couldn't take the phone away from my mouth to cry. There was complete silence except for the sound of me weeping.

"Can I meet you somewhere?" he asked.

I was distraught at this point so I just hung up the phone. While I was looking for something to wipe my face someone knocked on my window and I looked up to a police officer motioning to me to roll down my window.

"Are you alright, ma'am?" he asked. I shook my head yes.

"Okay, I just wanted to make sure you were okay," he explained nicely.

I looked at him again after wiping my eyes.

"Elliott Kani?" I said in shock.

"Juanita?" he exclaimed. "How have you been?" he asked excitedly. I wiped my eyes and jumped out of my car. We hugged each other tightly. I haven't seen him in almost five years.

Elliot was my first boyfriend and I just knew we were going to get married. I met him in the tenth grade and we had Precalculus together. It was the first day of class and he was new to the school. He walked into my classroom and all the girls began gushing over him except me because I had my eyes on Justin McClain who sat right across from me. Elliott said the first time he heard me speak he was drawn to me. Elliott sat across from me to my left and Justin sat to my right. Everyday Elliott would strike up a conversation and I could see Justin getting jealous, but Justin wouldn't ask me out. Elliott would always ask me out to eat or study, but I would say no. I didn't want to ruin any chances of hooking up with Justin hoping he would make his move. Justin just wanted to be chased. One day I finally said yes to Elliott and we met up in the library to study for an exam. While there I saw Justin walk by hugging Wendy from the track team. I was heartbroken so Elliott turned and asked me if I wanted to go to the school's

homecoming dance to make Justin jealous. I said
absolutely and we were boyfriend and girlfriend after
that night. We dated all the way up until college.

Elliot and I chatted briefly and he told me he was married
with three children. I immediately envied his family. I don't
know how we lost track of one another but life happens. He
saw that I was very emotional so we exchanged numbers
and he told me if I ever needed anything to just call him.

As he drove away I said to myself, "I would love to meet his
family."

CHAPTER 7

During the entire weekend with my sisters, I thought about Gwen and I found myself getting angry all over again. She had the audacity to attack me. I still don't know how to confront Dr. Brice about his relationship with her.

Long after my sisters went to sleep, I packed. While packing up to leave in the morning, I pondered my next steps with Dr. Brice. This weekend had afforded me the opportunity to reassess my life as a single, professional woman grappling with Aaron's death, Dr. Brice, Gwen, and possibly heading back to work. These thoughts were on rotation. I grabbed the small bag of popcorn I had stuffed in my bag and munched on it while I watched some tech videos to get my mind off everything. It was three in the morning before I fell asleep.

An early call from Taylor woke me up. The popcorn had spilled onto the floor and some was stuck to my legs and ear. I lay in bed for an extra ten minutes; thankful for the time I'd been able to spend with my sisters.

Taylor, Shanice and I walked out of the hotel and hopped into Shanice's car in silence. We knew our long weekend was coming to an end and now we were headed home to face reality. We laughed and cried some more the entire ride. I had a great time with my sisters. Unfortunately, three days weren't long enough. Taylor had a two-week training to attend and Shanice will be hooking up with the doctor from the hospital. If I pry then Shanice has the right to ask me anything about Dr. Brice. "I might inquire later," I thought and then chuckled to myself. I want to know what happened on her date and if she allowed the doctor to operate on her. I was ready to tell her about Kingston.

We hugged and kissed each other before I got out of Shanice's car. Until next time I thought as I watched her drive away. Dr. Brice kept texting me and had called me at least fifteen times but I refused to answer his calls. He knew I was going away with my sisters so I didn't feel I needed to answer his calls with an explanation. I'm not as angry as I was a couple days ago but I hadn't forgotten either. I reached into my purse to get my keys and I realized I had his office keys. They had fallen into a small side pocket in my purse. No wonder he kept calling me. If I had listened to just one of his voicemails I would've known. I laughed. I'll call him once I get relaxed. Maybe he'll want to come over? Okay so I'm over being angry. Now that I've arrived home and there's no one here, I find seeing him is better than being angry with him... and being alone.

I walked into the house and was shutting the door when I heard a commotion outside. I heard people yelling and car horns beeping. I quickly peeked out the small crack in the door so no one could see me and noticed it was the Harrys next door arguing again. I don't know why they just don't get split up or go to therapy. Geesh! At least once a week something is happening over there to raise an eyebrow. Maybe I should book them an appointment with Dr. Brice's colleague, Dr. Thornton. I heard he is an excellent marriage counselor.

I locked the door and leaned against it for a second and exhaled. I thought about my life and how things seem to be getting better. I've been sleeping the last couple of nights even after the death of my brother. I believe thinking about a man is normal.

I put my purse and overnight bag down and sprawled out on the sofa like it was my bed. I felt myself dozing off just before my phone rang. If the phone wasn't in my hand, I wouldn't have known it was ringing because it was on vibrate. It was a blocked number. This has to be Dr. Brice. I was about to answer it when the doorbell startled me. I dropped my phone when I leaped off the sofa to answer the door. "Who is it?" I asked as I unlocked the door. Before I could even open the door, Gabriel forced his way into my house. "What are you doing?" I yelled. I was trying to push the door closed but Gabriel was too strong for me and forced his way inside.

"I thought you wanted to see me?" he snarled nastily.

Who would've known he had issues? Well he is seeing a therapist so that was a red flag but that was after we established a friendly relationship. I am seeing Dr. Brice, too, but I'm not crazy like this fool is.

"Sit down right now!" Gabriel shouted, as he slammed the door shut.

I'm pretty good under pressure so I tried to remember every Law & Order episode that could relate to my current situation because I needed to know what to do.

"I will not sit down! What do you want?" I demanded.

"If you don't shut up and sit down, I will beat the life out of you," he said angrily.

I guess I wasn't moving fast enough because he rushed over and pushed me onto the sofa. I saw the rage in his eyes as he headed towards me. I submitted quickly hoping he would not hurt me. I flinched and crouched down because I was really scared. There was no pretending today. He began pacing the floor and I wasn't really sure if he had a weapon or not. I don't think he needs one because he is much stronger than I am.

"Oh, now you don't have anything to say?" he questioned me in a taunting manner as his spittle sprayed from his mouth. I felt nauseated by his saliva mist spraying on my face. I stayed silent waiting for him to disclose what I had done to tick him off.

He turned to walk away from me then he quickly turned back with his fist raised. I put my hands up to cover my face but they weren't strong enough to stop the blow. Gabriel hit me in my head instead of my face. The impact was so hard that I fell to the floor. The pain was so intense and excruciating, too. I wanted to cry, but I couldn't. I began to feel this numbing sensation over my entire head. I curled into the fetal position to protect myself just in case he wanted to kick me or keep hitting me.

"I want you bad, huh, you said! Yup, I sure do!" he sneered; mimicking what I had said in my car that day I forgot to disconnect our phone call.

"You think you can just play these games with me and I was going to be okay with everything?" he shouted.

"No," I whispered.

"Then why did you say it?" he yelled.

"How am I going to get out of this," I thought. The more I worried the worse my head felt. The room went silent. I wanted to look and see if he was still there even though I knew he was. I wish he would just leave or kill me. My thoughts were so loud I was hoping he heard them. I heard him walk out of the room. What was I going to do? Where was I going to go? I was too afraid to get up. All of a sudden, I heard him shut the bathroom door. Is he crazy? Do I get up or is he setting me up? Should I try to leave my house? He could have a gun and was just waiting to shoot me. I opened my eyes and could see his feet down the hall in front of the bathroom.

Just then I looked under the sofa and saw that my phone was ringing on vibrate. I went to pick it up to see who was calling but I ended the call after being startled by Gabriel's footsteps headed back into the living room.

"Get up!" he shouted. I was so nervous. I tried to get up but I found myself stumbling.

"Hurry up!" he shouted again.

"I can't," I whispered.

My head was throbbing. I didn't even finish my sentence before collapsing. I felt him grab my blouse and drag me away from the sofa! I can see and feel but I just can't respond. I think I have a concussion. I could hear my heartbeat and the pulsation from the head trauma I just sustained. I have never led him on, never kissed him or told him I liked him. It's amazing how many things ran through my mind in a matter of seconds.

"You are so beautiful and I want you," he stressed speaking through his teeth and breathing rapidly.

"Is there something wrong with me?" he screamed while pounding on his chest. "I'm a good guy," he boasted.

I beg to differ. How can he say all of these wonderful things about himself while he is here beating on me?

Suddenly he stood over me and began to rip my blouse off. "Isn't this what you wanted?" he said.

I shook my head no as tears streamed down my face.

"Why are you crying," he said worriedly. "What did I do to you?" he asked.

He put his hands over his ears and backed away from me into a corner of the room and covered his face with his hands while still plugging his ears with his thumbs. I can see he doesn't like to see me cry.

I could see Gabriel from where I was laying on the floor. He was shivering and mumbling something under his breath. I needed to keep him away from me and my crying was the magic bullet.

After a short while, crying was becoming very painful and I felt myself going in and out of consciousness. "I have to do something. I can't just sit here and cry all day," I contemplated. I'm not sure if I can stand up without falling, so I began to crawl to the nearest wall so that I could sit up. I finally made it. The wall might have been about three feet away from me but it felt like an eternity to reach it. I coughed and immediately felt dizzy. My eyes never left Gabriel though. He lifted up his head and he noticed I had moved so he got up and started walking towards me.

"Where are you going?" he said in a different voice.

He was huffing and puffing. Then he pulled my skirt off and I started kicking and screaming.

"He is going to rape me and there's nothing I can do about it," I believed. I am dealing with a psychopath.

"Please stop!" I cried out.

I couldn't believe I was actually able to utter those words. He stopped dead in his tracks and put his hands over his ears again and backed up. He went back towards the bathroom and I heard the bathroom door open. I cried louder and then the bathroom door slammed shut!

"This is my chance," I considered.

A couple of the buttons on my blouse were gone so I did the best I could to close up my shirt by tucking it in and under my bra. Between the blood still dripping from my head and the sporadic sharp pains, I managed to pull up my skirt that was wrapped around one foot. I don't know why I'm worried about having clothes on. I leaned forward from the wall and turned on my knees to try and get up. I felt really lightheaded as some blood trickled down from my forehead into my eye but I was determined to do something. I could hear Gabriel in the bathroom screaming and yelling. He's probably in there putting holes in my wall because I kept hearing loud thumps. I am terrified but it's imperative that I get out of here one way or another.

"Where are my keys?" I wondered as I scanned the room. My phone was under the sofa but the door was closer. I thought about it and did not want him to hear my keys rattling. I kept crying so he could hear me. I picked up my pocketbook and fumbled around until I found my keys. I gripped them tightly so he couldn't hear them jingle. I finally made it to my front door when I heard the bathroom door open, but Gabriel didn't come out. I slowly looked down the hallway and I could see the bathroom light but not Gabriel. I began to panic as I tried to open the door but it wouldn't come open. I was breathing so hard I was afraid he could hear me. I dropped the keys and I closed my eyes tightly praying he didn't hear that.

"Juanita," he said in a scary voice.

You know the voice you hear when you're watching a woman who is about to get beat up by her psycho lover... yeah, that one!

I reached down and grabbed my keys and put my hand on the door and turned it. I collapsed to the floor. I could see but I couldn't hear or speak. Gabriel stood over me. I could see sympathy in his eyes this time. Who was he now? He recognized that something was really wrong but he couldn't figure it out. He picked me up and my body went limp. I was in some type of paralytic state. He laid me on the sofa and sat next to me like a mother would with her sick child. Gabriel stroked my hair. He got up and a minute later he came back with a damp face cloth and wiped the blood off my face.

"I'm sorry Juanita," he said.

He continued cleaning off my face. I didn't know who he was this time. I'm sure he's suffering from schizophrenia. From the different mood changes, the crying, the weird voices and now he's acting like a parent I really believe my diagnosis is correct.

How does Dr. Brice do it? I'm sure some of his patients are very violent. I sure wish he were here right now. I would tell him that I love him. I would tell anyone I love them if they could save me from this deranged man. I was beginning to gain some feeling back. I lay still because I didn't want him to know I was able to move.

After Gabriel cleaned me up a little, he gently pulled my shirt from being tucked under my bra and then began to massage and kiss my breast. I was totally disgusted. This is as far as he was going to get. While he was focused on assaulting me, I reached over and grabbed the vase on the end table next to the sofa and hit him in the head and he fell to the floor. I don't know where my strength came from but it surfaced right on time. I got up and staggered to the door. I put my hand on the doorknob and it turned all the way. I opened the door and that was as far as I got before Gabriel grabbed me from behind. I mustered up as much energy to try and fight back but he was enraged. He threw me to the floor and smacked me a few times. I blacked out. When I came to, he was throwing my things around the living room.

"I love you!" he shouted.

"Why did you make me do this to you?" he hollered.

I didn't make him do anything. He loves me... I would hate to see what he would do to me if he hated me. I noticed my phone light was on under the sofa but I couldn't reach it. He was still breaking things, punching holes in my walls and yelling out random things.

"We could make beautiful babies!" he exclaimed.

I attempted to crawl to the door again but he noticed me moving. He ran to me and stood over me ready to hit me again. I was in for it now. I saw him raise his hand back and I closed my eyes tightly because I knew this was it for me. I waited to be knocked out but he didn't hit me. I was too afraid to open my eyes because I didn't want to see what was coming next. After a few seconds of high anxiety, I opened my eyes and saw Gabriel looking towards the door. I couldn't see who it was but I did see Gabriel fall backwards before I passed out.

CHAPTER 8

I heard someone say Dr. Newton so I opened my eyes. The nurse and doctor were whispering. I could barely hear what they were saying. I think they have something going on because the nurse kissed the doctor and then she giggled. The nurse turned to me and noticed that I had awakened. I could see the amazement in her eyes. She excitedly tapped Dr. Newton on the arm and he removed his hand from her butt. The nurse smiled and walked out. Dr. Newton slowly walked over to me.

"Hello Juanita, I'm Dr. Newton. It's good to see you are awake," he said with a smile.

"What happened?" I asked. My voice was very hoarse and raspy sounding.

"You've been in a coma for two weeks," he said.

"Is that why my head hurts?" I inquired.

"Yes, and you're very lucky because you sustained a very serious head concussion, a broken arm and two broken ribs," he explained. Dr. Newton began to poke and prod to make sure my vitals were good.

"Nurse Kerry will be back to help you get comfortable," he stated.

Dr. Newton left. About fifteen minutes later Taylor and Shanice came rushing in. Taylor and my eyes connected first. She was ecstatic to see I was out of my coma. Shanice immediately burst into tears. They hugged and kissed me as carefully as they could. In between all of the hugs and kisses, Shanice expressed how anxious they were to hear my voice. The tears began to pour out like Niagara Falls. I was overwhelmed with love and their concern. Taylor stated how she and Shanice were afraid that I wouldn't make it out of my coma. I hadn't realized I actually came out of the coma yesterday and that my throat was sore from the breathing tube they pulled out.

"What happened?" I asked.

Shanice looked at Taylor and Taylor looked at Shanice and then they both looked back at me.

"Tell me!" I exclaimed.

"Can we talk about this once you get home?" Taylor asked. I knew she was hiding something because she couldn't look me in the eyes.

My father had a way of bringing this reaction out of Taylor. I would ask her what's wrong and she would just put her head down and say nothing. She would be withdrawn for a few days. Taylor had that same look the day my father tied her up and made her sit in a tub full of iced water with all of her clothes on while he drank a pint of Smirnoff. That was just one of the stories in her diary that made me cry. She said it hurt more to keep this from me because she was afraid of what I might do if I found out.

Shanice whispered, "Juanita, we just want to make sure you're okay before we discuss what happened."

"Why?" I asked.

Taylor and Shanice looked at each other again and then back at me.

"This is about me!" I declared as my throat began to throb.

Shanice put her head down, too. My sisters are always trying to protect me from something, but I do not need protecting. I turned my head from them. I heard Taylor get up and walk out of the room. I turned around and called out to her.

"Taylor, why are you leaving?" I asked, hoping she would turn around but she didn't. I can't imagine what they could be hiding from me. What did I do?

"Let her go, Juanita," Shanice pleaded with me.

"Fine!" I said with an attitude as I turned my head in anger.

"Don't get upset," Shanice stated.

"Well tell me what's going on. Now!" I demanded.

"Gabriel is dead!" Shanice blurted out.

"What!" I said surprisingly. "H...h...how?" I questioned Shanice. I really tried to remember what had happened that night Gabriel went rogue but the details were jumbled. Shanice stayed silent. "But how?" I asked again.

Shanice was about to speak when Nurse Kerry walked in and ordered her to go into the waiting room.

The nurse told me to calm down. She checked my vitals and changed my catheter bag. Gross. Before leaving, Nurse Kerry gave me some more pain meds after I told her my ribs were hurting.

I waited for Shanice and Taylor to return but they didn't. I decided to try and get up on my own but my body was in so much pain. I felt like just giving up but I'm stronger than my mental state. If I'm going to get through this I'm going to have to forgive my father. I laid back down and faced the window and cried.

"I forgive you," I whispered. I didn't want to, but I had to.

I can't understand why this happened to me because I'm a good person. My brother is dead and now Gabriel? Did Taylor kill him? I couldn't control the tears of sadness that fell from my eyes and found a resting place on my hand that propped up my head. I heard someone enter the room but didn't turn around to see who it was. "Get it together," I scolded myself.

"Juanita, are you awake?" Dr. Brice asked.

"Yes," I sadly replied.

I was about to turn around but I really didn't want Dr. Brice to see me crying. How did he know I was here? Who contacted him? I heard him slowly walking to the other side of the bed where my face is facing. I was glad that he was here to see me but what I really want to know is who killed Gabriel. I'm not sure if Dr. Brice would be able to tell me what had happened that day, not unless Taylor or Shanice had told him.

"Juanita, look at me," he pleaded.

"What, Kingston?" I reluctantly responded and then looked up at him.

"What's wrong?" Dr. Brice asked.

"Where were you when I needed you?" I cried out.

He just stood there and looked at me with this blank expression on his face. "Just go" were the words on the tip of my tongue before I realized it was Dr. Brice that had killed Gabriel. I closed my eyes and slowly exhaled. When I opened my eyes Dr. Brice had moved closer to my bed.

"I needed to see you. I can't stop thinking about you." Dr. Brice said softly.

The vision of Dr. Brice wrestling with Gabriel flashed through my mind. Dr. Brice put his hand on my arm and started rubbing it. His touch was strangely reassuring.

"I've been up here every single day waiting for you to wake up out of this coma," he whispered. "It's okay if you're angry with me. It's even okay if you cry. But please, let me stay with you for a while," he asked earnestly.

I turned my head towards the door and closed my eyes again while I allowed him to continue to caress my arm. I could hear someone coming in my room so I looked up. There was another nurse that stopped at the doorway with her hands on her hip.

"Kingston Brice?" the nurse called out.

Dr. Brice turned around to see who was calling him.

"Hello Tiffany," Dr. Brice said.

"When you're finished here come over to the nurse's station so I can talk to you, please," she said nonchalantly. Nurse Tiffany then turned around and walked away.

The way she emphasized "here" was as if being with me was something he had to do rather than something he wanted to be doing. Dr. Brice acted as if Nurse Tiffany had never popped in. He pulled up a chair and sat next to me.

The pain meds started kicking in and I was feeling a little tired. Before I could shut my eyes, Taylor and Shanice walked in. When they walked in they saw Dr. Brice and I followed Taylor's eyes as they focused on his hand rubbing my arm.

"Dr. Brice is going to stay here with me for a little while," I told them.

"Ok, we will come back later," Shanice said.

I could tell Taylor wasn't too happy about it; however, it's what I wanted. I also hoped this would let her know that I really care for him. Taylor looked at Dr. Brice suspiciously before Shanice and she kissed me on the cheek and left. Dr. Brice didn't move from my side. The pain medication made me very tired but it was hard to sleep consistently with Dr. Newton and nurses stopping in to give me medication and checking up on me.

Three hours later I opened my eyes to find Dr. Brice sitting by my bedside doing something on his phone. I closed my eyes again and heard Nurse Tiffany stop at my door again to say she was leaving and asked Dr. Brice if she could speak with him for a moment.

"No," he said as he continued typing on his phone.

I opened my eyes and could tell he was annoyed but he was very calm in his response.

By the time I had fully awakened it was nightfall. The room was dark and empty, too. I turned my head to see the prettiest flower bouquet from Dr. Brice. He makes my heart melt. I really love fresh and assorted flower arrangements. The bouquet was filled with red roses, pink roses, pink lilies, pink alstroemeria and purple wax flowers. My nostrils were filled with the wild scents and aroma of an orchestra of dazzling fragrances. I love him...

Taylor, Shanice and Dr. Brice came and visited me every day over the last week. I even had a few visits from Uncle Charlie and Auntie Sophia. They poured so much love into me during every visit until it was finally time to go. All of their encouragement helped me through physical therapy immensely. I hadn't walked in over two weeks. There was no significant damage caused by the blunt force I sustained from Gabriel, which helped me to recover quickly.

It was finally time to be discharged and Nurse Tiffany was assigned to my release. She was dragging her feet to sign me out. I hadn't seen her since the last episode where Dr. Brice said he didn't want to talk to her and here she is with an apparent attitude. She strolled into my room and her facial expression was not pleasant at all.

"What are you to Kingston?" she indignantly asked.

I ignored her because it was none of her business. I probably would have told her if she had asked me nicely. I just sat and watched her take the IV needles out of my arm.

"Did you hear me?" Nurse Tiffany said after tearing my skin as she snatched the last IV out of my arm.

"Ow! What are you doing?" I screamed at her.

She quickly put her hand over my mouth. I continued to scream through her fingers so that I could alert everyone in this hospital because she can't be trusted. My arm was whelped and bleeding where she tore the tape off and the needle scraped my arm.

I pushed her away with all my might away from me and she stumbled. She regained her balance. She turned, pinned my hand down and told me to keep quiet. She was pressing on my ribs, which were in so much pain and made it hard for me to breath. I tried to wiggle her off of my good arm, but I couldn't. Finally, a couple of doctors and a nurse came running in and pulled her off of me.

One of the doctors restrained Nurse Tiffany and made sure she didn't come back into the room.

"Get out of my hospital" Nurse Tiffany screamed at me.

"You're a maniac!" I shouted.

Dr. Brice returned from packing the car with the things I collected while being in the hospital when Nurse Tiffany ran over to him in a panic.

"Look what she did to me," she exclaimed, showing him her ripped sleeve and a cut on her arm that occurred when I pushed off me. It was clear she was looking for sympathy from Dr. Brice.

"Get your hands off of me." Dr. Brice firmly said as he backed away from her.

Nurse Tiffany was shocked. "What have I done to you?" she questioned him.

"I'm pressing charges," I interjected.

Dr. Newton stepped in and demanded that someone tell him what had happened. I refused to let the situation go and Nurse Tiffany needed to be held accountable for her actions. What kind of power does Dr. Brice have over her?

CHAPTER 9

After everything was over and I was officially discharged, Dr. Brice insisted on driving me home. We stopped at the pharmacy, picked up my prescriptions and headed for my house. I'm not sure how long we were riding around but I was feeling a little sleepy from the pain meds I had taken earlier.

We pulled up to my door and I immediately had flashbacks. I was so nervous about coming home and being reminded of the brutal beating that had transpired there. I felt the anxiety attacking my body and my mind. With every thought, the uneasiness became more intense and my legs began to shake. I shivered as if I had just come in from a very cold winter's night without a jacket or shoes.

"I'm here with you," Dr. Brice comforted me.

He must have observed my nervousness so he held me for a minute or two until I was finally brave enough to walk into my home. He went before me and held out his hand for me to come in. I slowly walked in. I noticed that my house was clean. The holes were repaired and painted too. I didn't fully inspect every room but from what I could see that there was no trace of what had occurred here less than a month ago. I began to feel dizzy but I wasn't about to lie down before taking a much-needed bath. He asked me if I needed one of my sisters over to help me.

"No, I can handle it. I'm not handicapped... well kind of," I said jokingly.

Dr. Brice prepared a bubble bath for me. Once the bath was ready he closed the bathroom door so I could get undressed. I pulled my panties off and I tried to pull off my dress. The dress was almost over my head when I lost my balance and fell to the floor.

"Juanita, are you okay?" he asked standing on the other side of the bathroom door.

I could hear the panic in his voice, which made me more nervous. My arm was caught in my dress and I was nearly naked on the floor. I was so embarrassed but I needed his help.

"Kingston," I called out.

"Are you okay?" he asked again.

"I need your help. But..." I conceded.

Before I could tell him that I was naked he had already opened the door. As soon as he saw that I was naked he turned his head but that made it difficult for him to take my dress off.

"It's okay if you look," I said softly.

As he helped me into the bath he apologized repeatedly. It was my fault for telling him not to call one of my sisters to help. That's what I get for being so stubborn.

Once I was finished bathing, I called out for him to help me get dressed. He held the towel up so I could get up and he wrapped it around me. I was too exhausted to fantasize. I didn't realize I needed him to help me get dressed. It was more complicated than I thought.

As I lay in the bed, I tried to doze off, but my slumber was repeatedly interrupted with Dr. Brice coming back and forth to check on me. He put the TV on low so it wouldn't disturb me but it had the opposite effect. I could hear Steve Harvey hosting the Family Feud with his weird laugh; I just love it. It was tough to laugh but Steve being the host made it impossible for me not to laugh. Dr. Brice came into my room to make sure I was okay after hearing me laugh repeatedly. He ended up watching the Family Feud with me. After a few minutes of standing up he got in the bed with me. His body was so warm even though I was under the covers and he lay on top of the covers. He put his arm over my stomach. I immediately felt safe then my mind went to him seeing me stark naked.

"Juanita," he whispered.

"Yes, Kingston," I replied.

"I'm sorry about what happened between you and Tiffany," he said. I didn't know what to say. He paused. "She was my fiancé until she met my aunt," he continued.

"Who is your aunt?" I asked.

"Gwen, the woman from the elevator," Dr. Brice said.

"How come you didn't tell me this from the beginning?" I asked.

"She's my aunt, and I was embarrassed, Juanita," he replied. "She's unpredictable," he confessed.

He explained to me that his aunt didn't want to leave her abusive relationship. Every time she would come to him crying and complaining about what her husband had done to her it angered him. I immediately thought about my mother and how easy it is to tell someone what they should do when they are in a bad situation until you are in that same situation. I could sympathize with him and her.

"What happened between Tiffany and your Aunt Gwen?" I asked directly.

Dr. Brice explained how rude and mean Tiffany was to Gwen because Gwen wouldn't leave her abusive husband. Tiffany would constantly mention how Gwen deserved everything she got for staying with her husband. He went on to say how Tiffany would call Gwen stupid right to her face when he would have to pick up Gwen after an abusive episode. Tiffany just became abusive to Gwen and him out of nowhere. Dr. Brice said he had enough when he walked in on Tiffany telling her coworker that she wouldn't be surprised if Gwen's husband killed her. He instantly called off the engagement. However, Tiffany didn't take that very well and would randomly call him begging him to give her another chance.

As for his Aunt's situation, he said he's emotionally tied to her and sometimes gets so angry with her he would have to take a walk to cool off so he doesn't do something he would regret.

We stayed in the bed and talked until I finally conked out. It was an emotional day. It has been an emotional year. I felt closer to Dr. Brice today. He really opened up to me. He talked about his childhood and I witnessed him becoming emotional at times. I really valued his sensitive side because he wasn't afraid to show his emotions.

When I woke up the next day, he was gone so I just stayed in bed. There was still this sense of fear lingering. I was beginning to feel anxious until the doorbell rang and startled me. I buried my head in the pillow hoping whoever it was would just leave. Taylor and Shanice had said they would be over after work so I know it wasn't one of them. It was too early so I just laid in the bed with my eyes closed. The doorbell rang again. Whoever was at the door was persistent because they rang the doorbell again. It was louder than normal. I lifted myself up but I felt dizzy so I sat up slowly so I could catch my balance.

"Who is it?" I whispered.

"Edible Arrangements ma'am," the voice said on the other side of the door.

I looked through the peephole before opening the door. I grabbed the fruit bouquet and closed the door. It was colorful, it smelled delicious and it was quite lovely as I inspected it before sitting it down.

The fruit sat on the table for about an hour before I decided to read the card to see what funny things my sisters had to say. I pulled the card from the bouquet and slowly sat down to read it.

"Juanita, because I care for you, I specifically made sure every piece of kind fruit in this arrangement was something you would eat. This is how everyday will be if you would let me call you mine. I never thought I would be this excited about pleasing a woman. I am not sure how I am going to get through work today knowing

you are home and I'm here at work. I want to be right there to take care of your every need. This is how my father treated my mother and this is how I want to treat you. If it's okay, I will be there right after work. I LOVE YOU and I will be better to you than anyone you have ever been with. I will call you during lunch."

I gushed. That was so romantic. I wish my father had treated my mother this way. Although she was mistreated, she deserved nothing less than what Dr. Brice is offering to do for me. That thought made me emotional. As I wiped my tears away, I reached in the table drawer and pulled out my extra key.

I got up and opened the door to leave the key under the mat and there was a woman standing on my doorstep. I guess I startled her because she put her hand on her heart when I opened the door. "How may I help you?" I curiously asked the woman.

"I am here to cook and clean for you today," she answered.

"Are you kidding?" I replied.

"No. Dr. Kingston Brice hired me to take care of you today," she related.

I just wanted to be alone but I couldn't tell her no. After she had been in my house for about ten minutes, I was glad she was here. She cooked, tidied up and made sure I was comfortable. I was able to take a bath and then I lay down because my body was really sore. I let her have free range. I dozed off but was awakened by my phone. It was Dr. Brice. "Hello," I answered.

"Were you sleeping?" he asked.

"Yes," I said and yawned.

"I'm sorry, I'll call you later," he said.

"You don't have to hang up," I insisted. Dr. Brice didn't say anything. "Thank you for the fruit and also for the help," I recounted.

"I wish I could do more," he stated.

"Well, she took very good care of me and she was so quiet that I didn't even know she had left," I told him.

"That's what I like to hear. Can I come see you after work?" he politely asked.

"That would be nice," I said.

"Great, because there's something I would like to ask you," he replied.

He wants to ask me something? Well I want to ask him something too. "I have something to ask you too," I confessed.

"Really?" Dr. Brice curiously responded.

I hung up with Dr. Brice and picked at the fruit until I was full. After about twenty-five minutes I got up to get dressed. I know Dr. Brice doesn't care what I look like right now, but I do. I want to stay attractive for him. I walked out of the bathroom and I heard the door open. I was so afraid. I didn't realize how much mental trauma was caused by what Gabriel did to me.

"Juanita, where are you?" I heard Shanice call out to me.

"I'm in here," I yelled back after exhaling.

Shanice and Taylor both met me in my bedroom and flooded me with hugs and kisses. I love my sisters.

After all the hugs, Taylor immediately headed for the refrigerator where she found the fruit bouquet. She came walking back in the room eating a piece of chocolate dipped strawberry on a stick and stood in the doorway. "So, where did you get this from?" Taylor asked, taking another bite of her strawberry.

"Was it from your therapist?" Shanice asked but I kept silent.

Taylor folded her arms after taking the last bite and blurted out, "Are you seeing him?"

"What do you think?" I answered.

Taylor walked out of the room. Shanice took my hand in hers and squeezed it. "Ouch, what did you do that for?" I said as I let her hand go.

"You better not mess this up for Harold," Shanice said, glaring at me.

One day while I was with Harold, my sister Taylor had come over to borrow a pair of shoes for a dinner party she was going to. I met Taylor at the door to hand her the shoes when Harold yelled from the back, "Nita, get your stupid behind back here now!" I was so embarrassed because Harold didn't know Taylor was there.

"I'll be right there," I yelled back. Taylor was so upset she snatched me by my shirt and dragged me outside.

"If I ever hear him talk to you like that again I will!" Taylor said in a harsh rebuke.

She was so angry she couldn't finish her sentence. Taylor then grabbed the shoes from me. She was furious as she turned to walk away but then turned back to me and muttered, "I don't know why you let him treat you like this, but I can't make you leave that clown."

I stepped back just in case she felt like slapping me.

"Nita, don't make me come get you!" Harold hollered.

I eased back into the house as Taylor irately watched me until I was out of sight.

"Well?" Taylor probed, jolting me back to the present.

"Well, what?" I replied. I completely forgot what the question was.

"Stop it with the theatrics and tell us how you really feel about him?" Taylor said, demanding an answer.

"Did you guys have an opportunity to talk to Dr. Brice while I was in a coma?" I inquired.

Taylor and Shanice looked at each other and then looked at me.

"Why can't you just answer the question?" Taylor asked.

"Fine!" I exclaimed.

"We're not seeing each other." I said sadly.

"Sure you're right," Taylor said sucking her teeth. "Forget it."

"Juanita," Dr. Brice called out.

Shanice got up from my bed and said to Taylor, "I think we should go."

"Why, we just got here." Taylor stated.

"You don't have to go ladies," Dr. Brice stressed stopping at my door before heading to the kitchen.

Dr. Brice went into the kitchen and started cooking. Shanice peeked in the kitchen and then came running to my room with an excited look on her face. Shanice and Taylor looked at each other and did a silent scream. They were jumping up and down.

"Oh, Lord, I need to keep him in my life." I blurted out.

"Not if you keep playing hard to get," Taylor commented.

I can count on her to say what's on her mind. Actually, both of them will but right now Taylor is being the more vocal one.

"I'm afraid I might hurt him and besides I still don't know much about him. I don't know any of his friends, family or colleagues," I divulged.

"What is it exactly that you need to know?" Taylor questioned.

"All of what I just said," I said as I hunched my shoulders.

"Have you really given him the chance to open up to you?" Shanice inquired.

"Please stay for dinner ladies," Dr. Brice said as soon as he entered the bedroom.

"Exactly!" Taylor exclaimed.

No one said anything. Dr. Brice looked around the room. "I guess that means yes," Dr. Brice said and he headed back to the kitchen.

Taylor's left eyebrow went up as Dr. Brice turned and walked back to the kitchen. I knew what that meant. She was going to take this opportunity to ask him every question she could think of asking.

We all headed into the kitchen after him. Taylor and Shanice helped set the table. They made sure I didn't do much. We were sitting at the table laughing and waiting for Dr. Brice to finish cooking grilled swordfish on watermelon and spinach salad. It smelled amazing.

We ate and talked for about two hours. Taylor carried on as if she had known Dr. Brice for years. I was happy. After a while, I excused myself from the table so I could take a shower and lay down. Shanice came into the bathroom while I was taking a shower. She put the top toilet seat down so she could sit.

"You can't be alone for the rest of your life," she spoke in a calming tone.

"I don't want to be alone, either," I replied.

"And," she said with a long pause.

"And what?" I questioned her.

"You can't keep running," Shanice blurted out.

"Hand me my towel," I asked. I turned the shower off and took the towel. I wrapped myself in the towel and slowly opened the shower curtain.

"What if he's not like Harold?" Shanice said.

Before I could reply there was a knock at the bathroom door.

"Are you two alright in there?" Taylor inquired.

"Yes," Shanice replied.

Taylor just barged right in the bathroom.

"What's going on," Taylor demanded to know.

"She's afraid Dr. Brice will turn into Harold," Shanice blurted out.

"I don't have time to get caught up in another abusive relationship," I emphasized.

"First of all, he's not a jerk. He's cute and he cooked for you! It can't get any better than that," Taylor stressed with her hands on her hips.

They were making my head hurt by bombarding me with their thoughts and questions so I ushered them out of the bathroom. I went in my room to get ready for bed. Taylor could see that they weren't going to get the answers they were looking for.

"We're going to leave, Nita, but we're going to finish this conversation another time!" Taylor insisted. Once I was dressed, Taylor and Shanice kissed me and walked out of my room. After they walked out of the room Dr. Brice came to my bedroom door to check on me before he left.

"I will stay until you fall asleep if you'd like me to," he asked.

"Nice meeting you Kingston!" Taylor yelled out from the dining room.

Dr. Brice smiled and he looked so adorable, too.

"You have wonderful sisters," he said.

"I don't know what I would do without them," I responded as I lay back on the bed. "I'm very lucky!" I recounted. I closed my eyes and I felt myself falling asleep.

"Juanita, Juanita!" Dr. Brice shouted.

I opened my eyes to see Dr. Brice had his arm pinned against my chest. I couldn't move. I screamed and kept screaming until I couldn't any longer. I wasn't about to let him hurt me without at least screaming for help.

"Oh, no, not again!" I thought to myself.

Why couldn't my sisters just stay? I knew deep down inside that Dr. Brice would turn out like Harold. I just can't stop attracting these types of men.

My first year in college I met Jay. He was on the track team. I still hadn't gotten over Elliott but life didn't stop. Jay and I connected as friends right away. We would meet in the library on Monday, Wednesday and Fridays to study for our debate class. Then we ended up meeting at his house. It was just natural for us to start seeing each. We were the couple everyone wanted to be. We became inseparable until the day I went to the mall with my friends and didn't tell him. He called my house looking for me and my mother told him where I was. When I walked out of the mall he was waiting outside. He insisted I leave with him. He pinned me up on the side of the mall and grabbed me by my jaw so tight that he left a mark on my face.

He then said angrily, "The next time you go somewhere, I better be the first one you tell!"

I was distraught and afraid. When I came home in a frenzy my father saw my face and drilled me until I told him what had happened. That was the last I saw of Jay.

I closed my eyes praying this was a dream. When I opened them again Dr. Brice was looking right into my eyes. "Please relax, Juanita. I'm here for you," he said as he kept up his guard. Dr. Brice was trying to calm me down. "Everything is okay, Juanita!" he stressed. Carefully releasing me from his arms, Dr. Brice reassured me that I'd be okay. I gasped for air and began coughing. I was having a panic attack and he knew it too. "Everything is okay," he repeated.

I think I was the one being violent.

"I'm not going to hurt you," he said.

I sat up and held him tightly. How could I think he could be like Harold? I'm so afraid of being abused and neglected. "Please protect me, Kingston," I cried in his ear. "I'm afraid," I said as I choked up.

"Ok," he softly answered me.

It didn't faze him that his shirt was saturated from the flood of tears. He stayed with me and we talked until I fell asleep.

CHAPTER 10

I woke up the next morning and I relished in the beautiful and enlightening presence of the sun rays streaming through my window. "God really brought me through this tragedy," I thought to myself as I reflected on what happened.

I heard Taylor in the dining room talking on the phone so I got up and headed to take a shower.

"Hey, Nita," Taylor cheerfully said when she heard me walking to the bathroom. "I'll be here all day so just call me if you need help with anything," she said as she returned to her conference call.

Before I entered the bathroom I heard her tell the caller on the other line to hold on.

"He loves you, Nita!" she yelled as I turned to close the bathroom door. I didn't respond.

After I was dressed I left my room and hung out with Taylor in the dining room. We watched the news and played cards for a while. She wanted to talk about Dr. Brice but I didn't. Eventually, she went back to working so I walked out of the dining room and headed to my bedroom. I sat on my bed and cried. "Chime, chime," the sound of a text notification echoed. I picked up my phone to see who it was from and as I reached over to grab it, I noticed a little black bag on the side of my bed. It was lying down as if it had fallen back there. I was about to look in the bag when Taylor walked in my room and said, "I need that bag." I lifted it up from my lap and handed it to her. She had her phone attached to her ear as she gave me a weird little smile and walked out of my room. Hmmm... come to think of it, I don't think it was her bag because she would've said I need "my" bag. She took the bag, walked out of my room and continued her phone conversation. I went to my bedroom door to see who she was talking to.

"I have the bag. (Pause) I'm not sure if she looked in it or not. (Pause) Because," Taylor said.

I don't know why she was trying to whisper because she was never good at it. Taylor looked back toward my room to see if I was coming. I dipped my head back into my room so she wouldn't see me. I heard her continue her conversation so I slowly stuck my head back out the door hoping to hear something of value relating to the black bag.

"Look, when I walked in there, she had the bag in her lap. (Pause) I said I'm not sure. (Pause) Well I didn't ask her if she went in the bag. (Pause) I don't think she looked in it because she would have said so. (Pause) Okay, bye," Taylor said.

Who was she talking to on the phone? It had to be Dr. Brice or Shanice. Dr. Brice did say he wanted to give me something or maybe Shanice and Taylor were trying to surprise me. They're good for that.

I finally looked at my text message and it was from Dr. Brice. He was bringing over dinner tonight. I smiled, lay back on the bed and sighed deeply. I'm getting used to seeing him often but I don't want him sleeping here because this is not that kind of party.

The days seem to be running into each other and before I know it, I'll be back to work. I have a doctor's appointment tomorrow to make sure the healing process is going as planned. I slowly wiped one tear away and took a deep breath.

I heard Taylor coming towards my room. She stopped at the doorway and leaned on the doorframe. I waited for her to mention the black bag, but she didn't.

"Everything is going to be okay," Taylor reassured me.

Fine, if she does not want to mention the black bag, I will. As I was about to speak, Dr. Brice walked through the door.

"Hello," he called out.

"We're back here," Taylor answered.

We waited for him to come to my room. Taylor sat on my bed and Dr. Brice stood at the door with a smile on his face. Taylor looked at him with a weird look.

"What are these two up to?" I wondered.

He wouldn't disconnect his eyes from mine though.

"How are you feeling?" Dr. Brice asked warmly.

"I'll be in the other room," Taylor said as she got up from the bed.

I could see that Taylor wanted to talk to Dr. Brice.

"Let me grab the wine from my car," he stated.

"I'll come out with you," Taylor blurted out.

"Great! I'll be right back, Juanita," Dr. Brice said as he left my room.

At this point I didn't even care. I was glad to see Kingston Brice. I closed my eyes and inhaled. The aroma of his cologne gave me the warm and fuzzies. I got up from the bed and looked in the mirror and fixed my hair. I smiled as I looked at myself. I actually saw the happiness in my eyes for a split second. Dr. Brice really makes me feel good on the inside and outside. I fixed my makeup and walked into the kitchen.

As I began to set the table, I saw Taylor and Dr. Brice laughing as they entered the front door. It doesn't take that long to get wine out of the car but I didn't say anything.

"What are you doing?" Dr. Brice questioned me.

"What are you talking about?" I asked.

"Please sit down. I'll take care of everything," he insisted.

"Yup, just sit down and chill out!" Taylor chimed in.

"All right, but let me finish setting the table and I promise I won't do anything else," I stated. Once I was finished, I sat down because they were going to see to it that I would do nothing.

Dr. Brice had bought a 2004 bottle of Peter Michael white wine and sat it on the table.

"The food will be here any minute," he walked over to me and said as he had grazed my neck.

"You're spoiling me," I whispered to him as I reached for his hand before it left my body.

"Would you like a glass of wine?" he asked.

"With dinner please," I replied.

Shanice knocked at the door before walking in toting Chinese food. It's amazing how Dr. Brice had orchestrated everything to happen on time without me knowing. Shanice walked by me and gave me a kiss on the cheek and sat the food down. All three of them were acting as if they were a part of a catering team. I chuckled inside as I watched them work in tandem to prepare dinner. I feel so special.

It was finally time to eat. Dr. Brice opened the wine and poured me a glass. He stood up after he poured my glass and cleared his throat. I glanced over at Taylor and she had the biggest smile on her face I had ever seen. My eyes quickly shifted to Shanice. She held an anticipatory expression. She was about to cry.

Dr. Brice began to expound on his knowledge of wine. He poured himself a glass of wine after he had walked around the table serving my sisters. Upon finishing he sat down right next to me and reached over for my hand under the table. And just like that we prayed over the food and began to eat.

"I wish this wouldn't end," I blurted out. What was I thinking?

"It doesn't have to end," Dr. Brice looked at me and said as he pulled out his chair and got on his knee.

"Um, what are you doing, Kingston?" I asked in amazement.

This cannot be what I'm thinking. Well what else could it be? Nothing fell to the floor for him to pick up. There it was in the chair next to Taylor... the black bag!

Taylor stood up and I could see her eyes cheering. Shanice stood up right after and covered her mouth with one hand and fanned her eyes with the other.

"Will you marry me, Ms. Winfield?" he asked.

I really wanted to say yes but it wouldn't come out. Dr. Brice continued to talk in an attempt to convince me that he is the one.

"Nita, you're everything I've ever wanted. Your smile, your indecisiveness, the way you wear every single piece of clothing... especially your shoes, your enticing perfume, and I could go on," he said flattering me.

My eyes were filled with tears of happiness. I tried not to blink.

"I'm mesmerized by your almond shaped, pretty brown eyes," Dr. Brice continued. "Your skin is softer than butter and the raspy-ness in your voice is like melody to my ears," He said then cleared his throat.

Why couldn't he have said "all of this" months ago?

"Where have you been all my life?" he said rhetorically.

Oh, he was pouring the flattery on and I was soaking it all in like the beach's sun.

"In every therapy session with you I knew you weren't being totally forthright. You had so much to hide, just as I do. Only you had the courage to seek help but I hid behind my degree and career trying to help others when I needed help," he confessed.

The levee has been compromised. I could no longer hold back the tears. Dr. Brice paused for a second to wipe my tears away. Between the sniffling and eye blotting, my sisters were on the other side of the table eagerly waiting for my reaction.

"I need you to help me through my past. I need your love. I need you!" he said as he slowly blinked his eyes and took a big gulp.

The last "I need your love" was all I needed to hear.

"Yes!" I yelled. I began kissing him passionately. My sisters came running over and hugged us.

This engagement will actually bring my sisters and I closer together. I wonder what they all talked about while I was in a coma. I know one day Dr. Brice will tell me what happened in my house that night. Although I'm curious, I don't believe I'm ready for the details.

THE NEXT MORNING

I woke up to laughter the next morning after the proposal. I could feel the cool breeze that lightly grazed my uncovered shoulders. Kingston's cologne had enveloped the house. It was hypnotic. I kept my eyes closed as I listened to Kingston and my sisters in the living room sharing stories. I contemplated getting up to go join them but decided to lie in the bed and eavesdrop on them. I knew it wasn't a dream as I twirled my engagement ring with my thumb. I kept hearing my sisters giggling and then some sudden outbursts being quickly quieted with Taylor whispering, "Keep it down, Nita is sleeping."

"I have a good one for you," Kingston interjected.

He started off talking about his old college friend Kevin, and how he was trying to impress this girl named Misty.

> *"Kevin had just met Misty a few days earlier and arranged for the both of them to go out to dinner. In an effort to impress Misty, Kevin carried on about his Mercedes Benz and how he would take care of her if she were his woman. Blah, blah, blah blah... The day Kevin was to take Misty to dinner, he had ridden the bus to Vivian's, his*

mother's, job and took her car without her knowledge... yeah, that Mercedes S class was his mother's car. Kevin knew Vivian was at training, but what he didn't know was that Vivian's training was offsite and that she had carpooled with a coworker instead of driving herself. Kevin picked up Misty and took her to an upscale restaurant where the reservations were made. It just so happened that Vivian's training group had booked dinner at the same place," Dr. Brice recounted.

I propped myself up to hear the story clearer because I was anxious to know what happened to Kevin. Would his lies and deception catch up to him?

"Vivian noticed her car outside the restaurant as she was leaving because of her personalized license plate "READY". She looked up at the restaurant window and noticed Kevin with some woman she didn't recognize. Vivian decided to wait outside and wait for her detective friend, James, to come and pretend to arrest Kevin for car theft. James went into the restaurant and asked Kevin if he was driving the Mercedes

Benz with the license plate "READY". Kevin proudly said yes and that's why James proceeded to put Kevin under arrest. Kevin calmly told the officer that it was his mother's car because he didn't want to be embarrassed. Misty was shocked that it wasn't his car." Kingston carried on.

"You're a momma's boy?" Misty scolded him.

"I just wanted to impress you, Baby," Kevin replied.

"Impress me with the truth! I'm not that shallow!" Misty angrily said as she got up and walked out.

"Please don't leave, Misty!" Kevin pleaded with her, but Misty didn't hesitate to leave or even look back.

"That's what he gets, ole liar!" Taylor sneered.

"Vivian then took the car and Kevin had to find a ride home on top of that. When Kevin finally made it home, he found himself locked out because his mother had put the deadbolt on," Kingston added.

I heard them laugh and make fun of Kevin for his unwillingness to be honest to Misty. Kingston said. "Wow. Kevin's mother is my hero." I thought.

Kevin taking his mother's car without her knowledge reminded me of the day Shanice had taken money from my dad's wallet to buy her elementary school science project supplies that he had promised to buy. He was good at forgetting to do things but he never forgot to go out just about every weekend to get drunk. Maybe my mother was attracted to the crazy now that I think of. Grandma Mae's husband was a lot like my father, come to think of it.

Once my father sobered up later the next day, he apologized to Shanice for not taking her to the store. He wasn't a total demon all the time but that day he was Lucifer himself. Shanice told him that Ma had taken her to the store the night before because he wasn't able to. My dad went in his wallet to give my mother the money but Shanice interrupted excitedly, "It's ok, dad, I took the money from your wallet!"

My father's eyes turned dark red in a matter of seconds. He stared at the money in his right hand and slowly put the money back in his wallet. He clenched his teeth in anger as he held open his wallet. I thought he was going to put his wallet back in his pocket but he gripped one end tightly and raised his hand with the other end of the wallet flapping. He began whacking Shanice in the face with his wallet while yelling, "Don't you ever take my money without asking me!"

Shanice didn't get a word in edgewise to tell him that he told her to take the money because he was yelling and whacking... he was too drunk to remember anyway. She was backed into the corner with nowhere to run so every blow caught some part of her head or face. His wallet was full of plastic cards and receipts that went flying everywhere with each blow.

My mother went to grab my dad's arm to stop him, but he turned and pushed her. She stumbled across the room and bounced off the wall into the entertainment cabinet. She broke her arm and one of the cabinet's doors fell off from the impact. I saw the pain in her face as she grabbed her left arm with her right hand. I jumped as if to help her but I quickly stooped back down in the corner like a coward. I did not want to be a part of my father's abuse fest.

My mother had jumped up and grabbed a large figurine that was on the end table next to the chair. She held it up in her right hand and yelled, "Stop it, or I'll kill you!" My father turned and looked at my mother and he immediately stopped hitting Shanice. My mother wasn't playing. "Leave right now." she demanded.

"Put it down, woman!" my dad roared as he made his broadened shoulders even broader. But my mother held her ground. They stared each other down to see who would fold first. After about a minute, my father realized she was serious.

"You could try me if you want to," my mother threatened. My father quickly gave in. He knew she wasn't playing this time. I was afraid.

"You told her to get the money from your wallet, but you were too drunk to remember," my mother muttered in anger. My father put his head down, took his car keys and left.

My mother waited for about an hour after my father had left and called her cousin to give her a ride to the hospital. She kissed and hugged us all before she left us with her cousin's daughter.

"Put the deadbolt on and don't let anyone in... not even Jesus," *My mother insisted before closing the door. We knew what she meant. Call the police if my father tries to come home.*

I closed my eyes and exhaled. Before, that memory would have caused my heart to beat rapidly as I relived every single detail. However, this time it didn't. Forgiving my father liberated me from the resentment surrounding those painful memories. My next challenge is telling Kingston everything. I think I'm ready now.

"Juanita," Kingston said softly.

I gasped for air once I acknowledged him standing in my doorway. "Are you okay?" he asked as he moved to my bedside.

"I'm okay. You startled me," I replied tenderly with a smile.

He sat on my bed and pulled the frizzy pieces of hair out of my face. I could feel the warm air from his breath cover me.

"I just wanted to make sure my face was the first face you saw this morning," He said as he kissed my cheek.

"You're mine," he whispered...

CHAPTER 11

Kingston and I stayed on the phone all night last night. He serenaded me with two songs. Once he was finished, I grabbed one of my favorite books and read the first chapter to him. He said I was a great reader and should consider reading to children in my free time. I laughed. He's so encouraging. I never giggled so much. I wanted him to come over but it was best we communicated this way.

"Honey," Kingston said.

I didn't realize I had fallen asleep. "I'm sorry," I replied.

"Get some rest my love. I can't wait to see you tomorrow," he said before ending our video call.

Our wedding day is finally here. After dreaming of a ten person bridal party with four hundred guests in attendance, we settled on a small ceremony consisting of close family and a few friends. We rented a small hall to at least have the "real" wedding feeling. Although we could afford an elaborate wedding, we decided that we didn't need all of that. Getting married as soon as possible meant more to us. I still can't believe this is actually going to happen. From not being able to sleep, now I'm about to have someone that will be here sleeping next to me for the rest of my life. This is surreal. I'm extremely nervous about this life-changing event. I don't know what I did to deserve it but I'm running away with it. We can't turn back now because we both put our homes up for sale. We will officially move into our new home when we return from our honeymoon. We feel that in order to start fresh, we really wanted a new home that we could make ours.

I stood in front of the mirror in my lace panties and admired my body. "I really hope Kingston likes this," I whispered to myself as I turned to the side and looked at my butt. I sighed deeply. I walked over to my dress and ran my hand over the lace and beaded pearls that adorned it. The butterflies in my stomach continued to grow, as the time got closer to seeing him today. I was about to pull my wedding dress off of the mannequin and try it on for the tenth time when the doorbell rang. I darted over to my bed to put on my bathrobe. Who could this be?

"I'm coming? I yelled out.

I quickly tied my robe and went to the door. I know it's not Taylor or Shanice because they're not due to be here for another two hours.

"Is that you, Kingston?" I asked, but there was no response. Maybe my sisters are here to surprise me, I suspected. I unlocked the door, turned the knob and Harold burst in. I waited for someone to enter after him because he didn't close the door behind himself. My mind went back to my last encounter with Gabriel. I immediately began to feel threatened. I was in panic mode. I backed up from Harold to avoid any kind of strike he might take at me.

"Oh no, no, no. Not again," I uttered.

"Juanita, you can't marry him," Harold said. "You were supposed to be my wife."

Harold was pretty calm, but he is still unpredictable. He was sweating profusely as if he just ran a mile to get here.

"I love you, Juanita," he stressed.

I followed Harold's eyes moving down to my chest searching for a view of my skin. I clasped my robe together to secure its closure. There's no way I will afford him any pleasure. I have a restraining order on him but mentioning that would be useless because he has no sense of reasoning. There is no one here to save me. A million scenarios came to mind but none of them would avoid him from raping or harming me in any way. I could hear myself breathing heavily, which heightened my fear.

"Say something!" he shouted.

I jumped. I didn't know what to say. The tears began to fall one after another but I didn't take my eyes off of him. Harold started walking towards me. The more steps he made, I took twice as many backing up. I began to pray.

"I'm not going to hurt you," Harold insisted.

"Please don't yell at me again," I said firmly as I reached my bedroom door.

Harold extended his hands out for me to embrace him but I refused to. His countenance quickly changed. My reluctance angered him. He grabbed me by my shoulders and pulled me towards him. I screamed.

"This is my wedding day and I'm about to die," I thought.

"Let her go or I'll shoot!" a familiar voice echoed from behind Harold.

"Help me!" I yelled out.

Harold refused to loosen his grip. He turned around to see who was commanding him to surrender, which allowed me to see Elliott pointing a gun towards Harold's back.

"This is your last warning!" Elliott said as he cocked the trigger.

I held my breath and froze.

Harold turned back to me and whispered, "Please don't marry him." He then pushed me away from him and turned towards Elliott. I stumbled and fell backwards. I exhaled as I crawled backwards to get as far away as possible from Harold as I could. It was like a scene from my childhood. Harold roared in a rage and ran towards Elliott. I covered my eyes in fear of what I was about to witness. Two shots rang out like Sunday church bells. Then there was a loud thump. Harold fell to the floor.

"You shot me!" Harold exclaimed.

I ripped my hands from my eyes in utter shock. Elliott immediately requested a paramedic and called in the incident. Harold was holding his right leg. He was moaning in serious anguish. The gunshots were crippling. I was distraught and relieved that Elliott hadn't killed Harold. I cannot handle another death. Once Harold was handcuffed, Elliott walked over to me and helped me up from the floor. His embrace was comforting. He said he stopped by to tell me that he couldn't make it to my wedding because he was called into work. He stated he was going to call me but had this weird premonition to stop by instead. He was glad he did... so was I.

Within minutes two police cars pulled up along with the EMTs. They questioned me and processed the scene. Watching them shuttle Harold off in the ambulance with a police officer in tow reassured me that I was safe. Afterwards, I group texted Taylor, Shanice and Kingston to let them know what had occurred. Elliott made sure one of the other officers stayed with me until someone showed up. I expressed my gratitude and told him that I would have him and his family over for dinner soon.

I heard a car door slam followed by scurrying footsteps. Kingston ran into my house and found me sitting on the sofa with the police officer. He ran over to me and held me tightly. Right after the officer left, I recounted what had happened in detail. I was so glad he was here... he silently held me. Afterwards, Taylor and Shanice ran through the front door. They assembled around Dr. Brice and me. We held each other and cried. I exhaled.

We are six hours away from saying "I do" and I refuse to postpone the wedding. Nothing was going to keep Kingston and I separated. I've waited too long for this.

THE WEDDING

I walked down the aisle to the soft melody of *Here Comes the Bride* that filled the air, reaching the church's rafters. As I slowly passed by my Uncle Charlie, he smiled. I returned the gesture... oh, how he reminds me of my mother. I wish she were here to hold my hand or tell me that she approves of Kingston. I know she would be so proud. I quickly felt relieved that she wasn't here to celebrate. I didn't want her to be jealous or yearn for this kind of marriage that she never had. My eyes were becoming moist. I scanned the pews and connected with Myles. I silently prayed that he wouldn't have a dysfunctional childhood. I smiled and winked at him. My eyes left him and jumped to Gwen. "She better not get in the way," I thought. I smiled at her. I continued down the aisle until my eyes reached Kingston. He tilted his head and smiled. Then he put his hand over his heart and licked his lips. As soon as I reached him, he hugged me. The Minister cleared his throat, letting Kingston know that we were not married yet and to be respectful. Laughter rang out from our guests. The Minister read through the vows as he held the open Bible.

Once he got to the part where he asks, "If any of you has a reason why these two should not be married, speak now or forever hold your peace", I turned and noticed Taylor looking around waiting for someone to disapprove this marriage so she could show them to the door. Fortunately, no one said anything.

"I do," Kingston said. Then we kissed. I tried not to cry to the point where I'd end up looking like the bride of Beetle Juice.

We danced, ate, laughed, and were inspired by some of the speeches. I didn't realize how much I was loved. What I took away was that the trauma wasn't greater than love.

The wedding reception was finally over. We decided to stay at Kingston's house before leaving for our honeymoon to Jamaica in a couple of days. We pulled up to Kingston's front door and he jumped out to open the passenger car door. I stepped out of the car. We approached his front door and he opened it. He whisked me off my feet. Kingston carried me over the threshold and kicked the door closed once we were inside his house.

The moment I've been waiting for since meeting Dr. Kingston Brice was upon us. I wanted him to take complete control of me tonight. I belong to him in all the right ways. He carried me into his bedroom and sat me on his bed. I took a quick glance of the room. Red roses in glass vases filled every dresser and tabletop in the room. The bed was decorated with different colored rose petals. Kingston stood up, went to one of the dressers and took out matches. He walked around the room, lighting the candles that hung in sconces on the wall. When he was done, he came back and bent down in front of me. He slowly lifted up my dress and slid his hand down my right ankle and took one shoe off at a time. I rested my hand on his shoulder. We were silent. "What will he do next?" I wondered. He stood up and put his hand out to help me stand up. Kingston put his hands around my waist and pulled me into him. He began to kiss me. Everything was in slow motion. He withdrew his tongue from my mouth and began kissing my neck while unzipping my dress. His hands moved from my waist and up to my shoulders as he began removing my dress straps. My dress fell to the floor. I had nothing on except for a red thong. He reached his hand out for me to step over and out of my dress.

"You're beautiful, Juanita Brice," he said shaking his head in approval.

"Thank you, Kingston," I replied, waiting for his next move.

"Don't move," he insisted as he pulled his shoes off.

He didn't have to worry about me moving. He's running the show tonight. He took off his tux and lay it on the chair next to the bed. Standing still in his boxers he walked up to me.

"Can I touch you?" he asked.

"Yeah, what the heck are you waiting for?" I thought to myself. I shook my head yes. He reached out with his left hand and touched my waist then began kissing my breast for a bit.

He always starts at my waist. I like that. It's a safe place.

I felt his tongue graze my nipple and then my stomach down then my belly button until he reached the band of my panties. With his teeth, he wiggled them off. He ran his hands up the back of my legs until he stood straight up. Once his hands reached my waist, he pulled me over to the bed. I could feel his excitement as our bodies met. He pulled his boxers off and then lay on top of me. He slowly slid inside of me. My eyes rolled back in my head. He started slowly stroking. I tried to keep silent but I couldn't. I quietly moan. We both were breathing heavily. Suddenly he pulled out. He then lifted my body into his and picked me up. I didn't realize how strong he was. I've never experienced this kind of pleasure before. I held him tightly as he walked over to the bedroom wall next to the bed. He secured my back to the wall and pulled me on him. I lightly bit him. I felt pure ecstasy! My nails locked onto the skin on his back. I knew it turned him on more because his lovemaking became more intense. He let out this exciting grunt and stopped. He kept me suspended to the wall. I exhaled and wiped the saliva that leaked from my mouth... I had no control. I felt him tremble a little and then he exhaled. He kissed my neck and made his way to my mouth. Slipping his tongue in again. After a few seconds Kingston let me down. He released his body from mine and I tugged at his arm. It's my turn now…

THE END

Dear Readers... thank you for purchasing my book. After months of preparing this book for release I had you in mind throughout this entire journey. I'm grateful for your support and I hope you enjoyed Therapy Fix. Your support will afford me the opportunity to make the next steps toward publishing my next book.

If you enjoyed this book, I ask that you share it with your book clubs, family, friends, neighbors, and social media friends.

Feel free to email me pictures of you with my book or upload them to one of my social media sites. Also, please leave a book review on Amazon.

Blessings,
Helen Baskerville-Dukes

SOCIAL MEDIA

Twitter:	HelenBDukes
Instagram:	HelenDukes
Facebook:	Author Helen Baskerville-Dukes
LinkedIn:	Helen Dukes
Email:	HelenBDukes@gmail.com